LILA MAXWELL'S TO DO LIST

❑ Set up crucial meetings for Nicolas Camden—
my boss…and the man of my dreams.

❑ Try to get the memory of what happened
between Nick and me on his desk out of my
head.

❑ Discuss the future of Colette, Inc., with Nick—
leave our personal future out of it.

❑ Take home-pregnancy test…just in case.

❑ Return "magical" brooch to Rose—tell her she
may have been right about its powers of love,
although only time will tell.

Dear Reader,

Welcome to Silhouette Desire, where every month you'll find six passionate, powerful and provocative romances.

October's MAN OF THE MONTH is *The Taming of Jackson Cade,* part of bestselling author BJ James' MEN OF BELLE TERRE miniseries, in which a tough horse breeder is gentled by a lovely veterinarian. *The Texan's Tiny Secret* by Peggy Moreland tells the moving story of a woman in love with the governor of Texas and afraid her scandalous past will hurt him.

The exciting series 20 AMBER COURT continues with Katherine Garbera's *Some Kind of Incredible,* in which a secretary teaches her lone-wolf boss to take a chance on love. In *Her Boss's Baby,* Cathleen Galitz's contribution to FORTUNES OF TEXAS: THE LOST HEIRS, a businessman falsely accused of a crime finds help from his faithful assistant and solace in her virginal embrace.

Jacob's Proposal, the first book in Eileen Wilks' dynamic new series, TALL, DARK & ELIGIBLE, features a marriage of convenience between a beauty and a devastatingly handsome financier known as the Iceman. And Maureen Child's popular BACHELOR BATTALION marches on with *Last Virgin in California,* an opposites-attract romance between a tough, by-the-book marine drill instructor and a free-spirited heroine.

So celebrate the arrival of autumn by indulging yourself with all six of these not-to-be-missed love stories.

Enjoy!

Joan Marlow Golan

Joan Marlow Golan
Senior Editor, Silhouette Desire

Please address questions and book requests to:
Silhouette Reader Service
U.S.: 3010 Walden Ave., P.O. Box 1325, Buffalo, NY 14269
Canadian: P.O. Box 609, Fort Erie, Ont. L2A 5X3

SOME KIND OF INCREDIBLE

KATHERINE GARBERA

Silhouette Desire

Published by Silhouette Books

America's Publisher of Contemporary Romance

Special thanks and acknowledgment are given to Katherine Garbera for her contribution to the 20 AMBER COURT series.

 SILHOUETTE BOOKS

ISBN 0-373-76395-6

SOME KIND OF INCREDIBLE

Visit Silhouette at www.eHarlequin.com

Printed in U.S.A.

Books by Katherine Garbera

Silhouette Desire

The Bachelor Next Door #1104
Miranda's Outlaw #1169
Her Baby's Father #1289
Overnight Cinderella #1348
Baby at His Door #1367
Some Kind of Incredible #1395

KATHERINE GARBERA

lives in Central Florida with her husband and their two children. She wrote her first book to prove to herself that she could do it and to have something to read at work! She believes firmly in fiction that reflects the reality of her life and the lives of those close to her. She is a past recipient of the Georgia Romance Writers Maggie Award. She loves to hear from readers, and you can write her at P.O. Box 1806, Davenport, FL 33836 or e-mail her at kgarbera@yahoo.com.

To secretaries everywhere who do an impossible job
with very little thanks, but especially to those I work
with at Disney Event Productions:
Gina McTigue, Joyce Campos, Adele Swearingen,
Eva Artimovich, Mary Leppich, Mary Baker,
Becky Latourelle, Karen Satre and Kelly Darden.
Also a special thanks to those women who mentored me
when I was young and green! Vita Charles,
Cindy Michener, Shirley Colebank and Jackie Mathews.

One

Late again, Lila Maxwell thought as she hurriedly closed the door to her third-floor apartment. She loved her home. It wasn't much, a four-room apartment in an older but nicely kept building. She'd spent the last two years carefully decorating each part until her flat of rooms had become her dream home.

She ran down the stairs at a rapid pace because she liked the exercise. As an administrative assistant at Colette, Inc., the world famous jewelry company, Lila spent most of her time sitting. The early morning was dark and Lila longed just for a minute for the warmth of her native Florida. Youngsville, Indiana, had a great community, but the weather was sometimes too cold for this Florida girl.

"Lila, can you stop for a cup of coffee?" her land-lady, Rose Carson, asked, stopping Lila in her tracks.

"Rose, I wish I could, but Nick's due back today and I'd like to be in the office before he gets there." Nick Camden was her boss. And the man of her dreams.

Not the girlish fantasies she'd entertained of a white knight who rescued her from the small government-subsidized duplex she and her mother had shared, but womanly fantasies of dark passion with a man who saw her for more than a nice collection of body parts. She flushed a little and hoped Rose didn't notice.

"I have something for you. Wait here for a minute," Rose said.

Lila loved her landlady. She was kind and caring and had made her feel at home when everything around her was very foreign. Rose's apartment took most of the bottom floor. Warm and inviting, it made whoever entered feel that a caring, successful woman lived there. Lila hoped to create that for herself some day.

"Here it is, Lila."

Rose handed her a beautiful piece of jewelry. A brooch made of amber and precious metal. It was almost heart-shaped and, though the term seemed inappropriate in the presence of something so precious, it was pretty. As Lila fingered it gently, she knew she shouldn't wear it. "I can't take this."

She handed it back to Rose, but the woman refused to take it.

"Just borrow it for luck."

"Thank you, Rose, but no. This is too valuable."

"I want you to wear it. It needs to be on a pretty young lady."

Rose brushed aside Lila's coat and fastened the brooch to her suit jacket. Lila loved the brooch but she knew better than to take something this valuable. She tried to remove it, but Rose's hand covered hers.

"Lila, it would mean a lot to me. It brought Mitch and me together. I like to think it brings love to the lives of those it touches."

Rose got that misty look she often had when she spoke of her deceased husband, Mitch. Though her black hair had a few shades of gray, Rose was still attractive. Her figure was slim but slightly rounded, giving way to a more matronly style of dress. Unwilling to upset her neighbor, Lila decided to keep it for today and return the brooch tonight.

"Thanks, Rose. It *is* lovely. I have to go," Lila said with a glance at her watch.

Rose nodded, and Lila hurried out into the cold. The sun was breaking over the horizon. It was nippy but not too cold for a walk to work. She lifted her face to the sun and pretended the high for today wasn't only fifty degrees.

She loved the parks and trees full of fall colors. Yellows, browns, oranges and reds filled every space. Halloween, her favorite holiday, was right around the corner, she thought, attributing the extra bounce in her step to excitement.

Usually she had some company on her walks to work. Sometimes Jayne and Sylvie walked with her, but Jayne had recently gotten married and hadn't been up so early in the mornings. And today she was too early for Sylvie.

Lila liked the fact that she had good friends here. It was as if she'd found the surrogate family she'd always been searching for. She really loved her life in Youngsville.

Not wanting to be late on Nick's first day back, she hurried. In her purse was the banana bread she'd baked last night. In fact, she'd spent every night for the last week baking.

Lila always felt in control in her kitchen. She was the executive there and she knew her way around. It was easy for her to fool herself into believing that Nick Camden hadn't almost kissed her while she was kneading dough and making sheets of sweet rolls.

A car slowed behind her. The low purr of an expensive machine told her it wasn't one of the other Colette, Inc. secretaries offering her a ride. She kept her head down and walked. She wasn't prepared to face Nick outside the office. In fact, he'd passed her a hundred times this summer and never once stopped to offer her a ride.

Men want only one thing from women like us, Lila. Her mother's warning echoed in her mind. Her ex-boyfriend, Paul, had proved her mother right. She didn't glance toward the car despite the warmth emanating from the open window.

"Want a lift, Lila?"

"No, thanks, I'm enjoying the crisp morning." If only she could stop shivering.

"Liar," he said, not unkindly.

He was right, she was lying. But that didn't mean she was going to admit it. A car honked, and Nick waved the driver by. Lila wasn't getting in the car with him, because after last week she didn't trust herself. She'd spent all of her time in Indiana adjusting to the new community and her home, learning to be proficient at her job and making some casual friends. But she hadn't been prepared for Nick Camden's sexy gaze when he had turned it her way.

She'd dreamed of him kissing her and touching her, but when he'd leaned closer to her last week in the office, she'd frozen. Paralyzed with the fear that she would disappoint him, she'd backed away. But he had a gleam in his eyes that said retreat wasn't possible. *Damn him.* She tried to give him a reassuring smile and walked on. "Thanks, but no thanks."

"Suit yourself, Florida girl, but it's a cold morning and my car is warm and comfortable."

He was temptation. He hadn't been when she'd first started at Colette. But lately she'd been looking for a man who'd be serious with her. A man who wanted kids and a nice house. A husband who understood the importance of family.

Nick didn't even register on her scope because he

changed women every week. He wasn't a playboy, but he never seemed content to stay with one woman. He was like a hungry wolf eating his fill and moving on. Lila wasn't interested in being his next meal. If she thought there was even a remote possibility that Nick would stay with her, she'd give in to him.

But there wasn't.

Almost two years ago she'd decided that Indiana was a place for fresh starts. She wasn't going to get involved with any man unless she knew for certain it was right. Which meant no Nick Camden. No matter how heavy he made her blood run.

"Lila, I've been out of the office for a week. I need you to brief me on what's been going on."

Maybe she'd misinterpreted his intentions. She shrugged, and finally gave in. "Okay."

She prided herself on being a good secretary and before the episode last week she'd never have hesitated to get in his car. He didn't scare her on a conscious level, but her mind warned her to be wary of him. There was something about this very sophisticated man that wasn't very civilized.

She slid into the plush leather seat and hurriedly fastened her seatbelt. She closed her eyes, letting the heat seep into her bones. A warm masculine scent surrounded her and she imagined Nick leaning over her. His breath brushing her lips.

Wait a minute!

Her eyes flew open and Nick's face was a scant inch from hers. There was something electric in his eyes. Something that made her pulse race and her breasts tingle. Something masculine that called to every female instinct buried deep inside her. Made her want to indulge senses she kept firmly under lock and key, let them out and experiment with this very experienced man.

"Nick, what are you doing?" God, she could barely speak. She wanted to lean forward and taste him. To see if the sin his wicked mouth promised was as delicious as her fantasy assured her it would be.

"Fixing your seatbelt. It's twisted."

She couldn't breathe as his fingers brushed against her breast. Her nipple tightened and she wanted to thrust her chest out so that he'd have to do more than accidentally caress her hungry flesh, but instead she bit her lower lip.

"There we go," he said.

He pulled his hand away slowly and she wished she could see his eyes behind those dark sunglasses he wore. Nick was a master at seeming in control, but his eyes always gave him away.

Her pulse was still racing and she wanted to pull him back to her, wanted to feel his hard body pressed to her own softer one. Maybe Rose's pin was working its magic, spinning a spell around Lila and her dream man.

Lila shook her head. If Nick wanted her it was for business and not in the way a man wanted a woman. He was too savvy to mess up a winning partnership with old-fashioned lust.

Nick put the car in gear. Sweat broke out on Lila's body but it had nothing to do with the heat coming from the car. It had to do with the man sitting next to her. A man that she'd decided was off-limits. A man, she suddenly realized, who'd decided she was his next meal.

Nick knew that he'd unnerved Lila, but he couldn't just drive by and not stop for her. It bothered him that he'd probably passed by her this summer without noticing. But not that much.

He'd never paid much attention to her as a woman except to note that she complemented him nicely, being blond and built. She made them look good when he had visitors or when they attended meetings together. To him, Lila represented the perfect office assistant, someone who knew her job but was also pleasing to the eye.

All of that had changed after he'd returned from Paris in early September. Lila had seemed softer somehow. She'd chatted with him casually before taking a memo and he instantly knew something was different. Actually he knew exactly what had changed.

His reaction to her.

He'd gone on point like a hunting dog scenting prey, and he'd been unable to shake this damned attraction to her. And she seemed oblivious, which made him want to get a reaction out of her even more.

"You were going to tell me about your trip," she said.

Yeah, Camden. Now that you blackmailed her into your car, talk business. "I need you to prepare a presentation for the domestic guys with last quarter's financials. I have the data in my briefcase."

"I'll clear my desk and work on it first thing."

Nick nodded. Silence built in the car, and he realized he knew too little about Lila outside of work. He had no idea how she spent her free time. Lila was so homey sometimes he was amazed she'd chosen a career over a family. But she had. And now he wanted—no needed—to know why.

"You live at Amber Court, right?"

"Yes, why?"

"No reason. Do you like it?"

Oh, God, he sounded like an actor in a bad sitcom. He'd never tried to get to know someone he already knew. It seemed his MO needed a change but his focus on Lila was now purely physical.

"It's nice, but I've dreamed of owning a two-story house with—"

"A white picket fence, right?"

She bit her lip and stared out the window.

He knew he'd sounded sarcastic, hell, he couldn't help it. Reality was hard and cold when you spent most of your time in the dream world. And it seemed Lila Maxwell did a lot of dreaming.

Bothered that he'd hurt her, Nick changed the subject. He was not in the business of fixing hurts. He'd learned not to care after Amelia had slipped away from him into a drug-induced coma that was her only escape from the pain her cancer-ridden body felt— 24/7.

"How was the office while I was gone?" he asked, trying to sound casual.

At first, he thought she wasn't going to answer. She glanced over at him. She fingered her scarf with her pearl-pink colored nails and the image of those fingers on his thigh imprinted itself in his head.

"Not busy. A few more rumors than usual."

Focus, man. "What kind?"

She smiled, and his inseam felt tight. Damn, but she caused a reaction that was close to nuclear in him.

"Oh, you know, the ones where we're all booted out the door."

"You think they're unfounded?" Nick asked. He'd been hearing similar things overseas.

"I work close to the top and we haven't heard anything substantial, have we?"

Nick sighed and grunted. The turn into Colette, Inc. was busy with employees all arriving at work, and though it didn't require his full concentration, Nick gave himself to the task. He didn't look at Lila again until he'd pulled his Porsche to a stop in the spot designated as his. He hoped for once that Lila's sharp mind would miss his non-answer.

A quick glance at her showed she hadn't. He pulled his keys from the ignition and reached for the door handle, but her hand on his arm stopped him.

"Have we, Nick?"

Lying went against the grain. Nick believed that life's little lessons were best served cold. But Lila's heart was in her big brown eyes and she looked scared. Though it had been a long, long time since he'd wanted to protect any woman, he suddenly didn't want to shake Lila's world.

He faced her and leaned close.

"Not yet."

"That isn't a no," she said quietly.

The confines of the car put them so close together that he could feel each inhalation of air she took as she breathed. Staring at her pink lips, Nick wondered idly if his breath was now filling her lungs, filling her body with life, and he had the urge to fill her with something more real. He didn't want to be satisfied with the fact that their appearance impressed vendors and visiting executives in the office. He wanted them to be together, physically.

Nick knew on a basic level that he was trying to hide from the fact that his safe haven, Colette, Inc., had turned into a battleground, but it was more than that. He leaned closer to Lila, not stopping until he could taste the air she was breathing, her lips softening under his, her hand on his arm clutching helplessly at his sleeve.

He knew that he was in for a world of hurt if he pursued her this way. But the world had gone crazy, and the carefully sheltered life he'd built for himself was crumbling. The only thing that looked solid was Lila Maxwell.

Lila moaned deep in her throat and opened her mouth under his. All thoughts of keeping things light and simple vanished. His blood roared in his ears, and his body screamed for more. Her mouth was soft, warm, wet…welcoming on this cold October day.

She clung to him as if the moment had taken her by surprise, too. Her tongue responded shyly to his. It had been forever since a woman hadn't thrust her own tongue into his mouth before he'd even wanted her there.

Nick pulled her closer, groaning when the gearshift ground into his hip. He pulled away. "Damn."

Lila stared at him as if she'd never seen him before. Her lips were swollen and her face was flushed. Tendrils of her perfectly styled hair surrounded her heart-shaped face. She was mussed and he wanted her more so.

He wanted that glorious hair spread on his navy pillowcase, those rosy lips swollen from his spent passion. He wanted his sweat and hers drying on their bodies. But he knew he couldn't put the car in Reverse and take them both to his home where they could spend the day in his king-size bed.

"Damn."

"You already said that."

"Some things need repeating."

Her hands trembled as she tucked the escaped

strands back into place. "What happened here, Nick?"

"I want you, Lila."

"Because of work?" she asked, not looking at him. Instead, she pulled her compact from her purse and repaired her lipstick.

Her armor was back and the dewy woman who'd been next to him just a minute before was gone. In her place was his ultra-efficient secretary. And he resented that. He couldn't pull out a mirror and makeup and smooth away signs of passion as easily as she had. "Because of you."

She gulped. "I'm not ready for this. I still think of you as my boss."

"Well, start thinking of me as your man."

He opened his door and got out. The air was cold but didn't cool the heat flowing through him. He wasn't going to be able to focus on anything in the office except that his wide cherrywood desk was big enough to support the weight of one slender blonde.

Lila met him on the sidewalk and brushed past him. He stopped her with a firm hand on her arm.

"What's the hurry?"

"I don't want anyone to see us coming in together."

"Don't be ridiculous. At least five people saw me pick you up this morning. And even more saw us pull into the parking lot."

"True. But I don't want anyone to get the wrong impression."

"Are you really that concerned with what others think?"

She nodded.

"Don't be. They aren't worth your time."

"You only say that because it's always the woman who comes out sounding like she's easy."

"Trust me, Lila, the last thing you are is easy."

"I know that, but other women…"

"If anyone says anything to you, tell me and I'll silence them."

She smiled. "Like Hannibal?"

"No. Like Dirty Harry."

"Death?"

"Intimidation."

"You're not as scary as you think you are."

"Neither are you."

"I'm not trying to scare you," she said and walked quickly inside the building.

But you are, he thought. Because a part of him was afraid she'd mean more to him than any of the brief affairs he'd had since Amelia's death two years ago, and that wasn't in the cards.

Two

The buzz around the office was that Colette, Inc. had a new board member who was planning on making some changes at the top. Lila returned from a quick clerical meeting led by Suzy, the Administrative Assistant in Human Resources, not feeling as upbeat about her job as she had a day ago.

She stowed her purse and tried to concentrate on her work, but the presentation she was creating couldn't hold her attention.

Dammit!

"Can you come into my office and take a memo?" Nick asked. Anger seethed around him in a cloud. He looked dark and menacing, not like the man who'd been keeping her at arm's length all day.

Lila saved the file she'd been working on and nodded. She tried not to glance at him as he hovered near her desk. The spicy scent of his cologne surrounded her and she breathed deeply to inhale his scent into her bones.

Bracing his big hands on her desk, he leaned over. His deep-blue eyes usually held boundless energy, but today anger simmered in their depths. She felt it radiating off him in waves. Concerned, she started to rub his hand, to offer him the most basic of human comfort, but then pulled back.

She watched as his eyes left hers to stare at her small hand now only a few inches from his right one on the desk. He'd spent the entire afternoon with the board of directors and, if his body language was correct, then the rumor that Colette was the object of a hostile takeover was true.

Colette, Inc. had proven a safe place for her to build her career and save the money she needed to buy her dream house. The rumored takeover reminded her how much she hated change.

When she'd packed up and moved to Youngsville it was with the intention of staying here forever. First, Nick had started acting like she was the most scrumptious woman he'd seen in years, and now her job was threatened.

It wasn't so much her role in Colette she worried about losing. It was her apartment. The homey place at Amber Court had given her the grounding she needed to find her own feet, to shape her own image away from her mother. And suddenly that looked as if it might be taken away.

"What's up?"

"I'd rather not discuss it out here."

Her stomach clenched, and she felt much the same as she had on that day in high school when the guy she'd been waiting for three years to be asked out by had told her that he'd only done so because she was considered easy.

"I'll be right in."

Nick straightened and then deliberately brushed his fingertip over the back of her knuckles. Her breath caught as electric tingles pulsed through her body. She'd spent so many hours at her desk wondering if she'd just imagined his attraction to her, but now she knew it wasn't a fantasy.

For a tense moment they stared at each other. Lila's breasts felt full and her lips were suddenly dry. She licked them. Nick tracked the movement and started to lean closer to her.

Down the hall an office door closed loudly. Nick stood and walked into his office without another word.

"Oh, my God!" Lila said. She had to transfer out of this office before she completely lost all of her common sense. She fingered the brooch Rose had given her before she left for work. It was beautiful, and Lila had found herself taking it off to look at it several times today. In fact, it seemed to glow a little more brightly whenever she touched it. Rose had said it had always brought her luck. Lila had the feeling she needed more help than this brooch could bring her.

She signed out of the local area network, or the LAN, and removed her laptop from its docking station. Nick's office overlooked Lake Michigan. Tonight, the view was dark and menacing. Being a Florida girl she didn't care for all the cold weather, but the changing leaves had been beautiful. After a year and a half here, she still hadn't acclimated herself to the Indiana weather.

Lila set her laptop on the corner of Nick's desk. He was hunched over his own computer, probably checking e-mail, she thought. Tension radiated from him, and she wanted to touch him, to massage those broad shoulders until he leaned back in his big executive chair and smiled at her.

Of course, he never really smiled at her. Sometimes when they'd completed a really tough project, he'd give her one of his half-smiles, and she'd feel a deep longing inside to make him really happy. But she never did. Sleeping with the boss was the one thing she'd never do. Except this morning things between them had changed. Her dreams were slowly becoming reality. The actions she'd always longed to take were now presenting themselves to her.

"Ready, Lila?"

She swallowed and blocked her train of thought. "Almost."

She powered on her computer. "Should we close the blinds?"

"Why, afraid someone might see us alone together in here?" There was a biting edge to his words.

"Not afraid exactly." She'd never been afraid of any man since most of them turned and ran when life got tough. She knew she was strong and could take all they had to give. But she always tried to keep a part of herself secret. And Nick was harder to hide from than anyone else.

"Trust me, Lila. Everyone knows your reputation. Anyone who might see us will know we are only working."

Stung, she busied herself at the computer, pulling up the company memo template and readying herself to do her job. His words shouldn't have hurt, she thought. After all, their relationship was that of boss and secretary. But the words did hurt.

"I'm ready, Nick."

"Lila…"

She glanced up, hoping he'd attribute the tears in her eyes to the late hour.

"Never mind."

They'd been carefully treading around one another since that night two short weeks ago when Jayne had interrupted a moment that had almost gone too far. She'd wanted so badly to taste his lips on hers. To feel that rock-hard body that he worked at keeping in shape pressed against her own. To experience for once in her lonely little life the touch of real passion.

"The memo should go to all staff in the Marketing Division."

"Just our team or domestic, too?"

"Domestic, too. I'm handling this announcement."

"Promotion?" she asked hopefully.

"I wish it were."

"Subject?"

"Grey Enterprises," he said, pacing across the room and stopping in front of the Zen rock garden that he adjusted every day or so.

Uh-oh, she thought. Nick's deep-blue eyes reflected the frustration and anger in his tone.

"Dammit," he said under his breath.

"Nick?"

"Have you heard the rumors of a takeover, Lila?"

"Yes, but I'm sure they are unfounded."

"They aren't."

Shock rumbled through her, and for a minute she saw herself back in that duplex she'd grown up in. The government-subsidized housing that had been her world until she'd gone to trade school and accepted this job. She saw herself back in that world she'd struggled so hard to get out of. She saw her dreams slowly dying and vowed that she'd do whatever it took to prevent that from happening.

"What the hell should I say to the staff? Don't worry, we're not going to let you lose your job?"

"I don't know. Is that true?"

"Hell, I wish I knew."

Lila's hands started to shake and she realized that

this wasn't just change happening around her. This
was the sky falling in. This was—

"Don't worry, Lila. Clerical staff is hardly ever let
go. VPs on the other hand..."

"No one's going to fire you, Nick."

"Lila, sometimes you are naive."

She wanted to argue, but knew that to a suave sophisticated man like Nick Camden, she must seem a
little small townish. "But the board loves you."

"We might have a new board member."

"Grey Enterprises?"

"Yes. Marcus Grey, their CEO, has bought eight
percent of the common shares on the market. He is
now the fourth-largest stock holder."

"What are we going to do?"

"Whatever we can to survive. I've worked too
damn hard to give this up without a fight."

He still stood with his back to her, searching, it
seemed, for answers in his Zen garden. She stood, set
her laptop on the chair and crossed to him. All her
protective instincts told her to cradle this man in her
arms. To comfort him and draw strength from the
comfort he could offer her.

She knew it was dangerous, though. Nick held her
dreams captive, what would happen if she gave him
the keys to her reality?

"What can I do to help you?"

He pivoted on his heel and faced her. His deep-
blue gaze brushed over her, and when he spoke his
voice was huskier than usual. He moved a few paces

closer. She could feel his body heat and started to back away. But something in his eyes challenged her to stay where she was.

"For me personally?" he asked.

For work, she wanted to say, but knew that wasn't true. Her words caught in her throat and she could only nod.

"Let me hold you."

She wasn't sure he'd really spoken. It was just like the dream she'd had the night before, in which he'd asked her to come into his office and then made passionate love to her.

"What?"

"I know all about sexual harassment and this has nothing to do with your job."

"Just hold me?" she asked.

"No," he said.

She waited.

"I'm going to kiss you, too."

She didn't hesitate to close the gap between them. She knew he was reaching out, as everyone in the office had been today. Just searching for some comfort in this time that had become troubled. But deep in her heart, as he lowered his head, Lila hoped it meant something more. Just a little bit more to him.

Nick knew that he was manipulating the situation, taking advantage of Lila because she was weak and vulnerable right now. But he'd wanted her for a long time. He didn't look too closely at himself because he didn't want to admit he had any of those feelings. The last time he'd felt this shaken was when Amelia had been diagnosed with cancer.

He brushed her lips lightly with his. She tasted like a bittersweet fruit and he wanted more. She sighed as his tongue slid past the barrier of her lips and teeth, learning the inside of her mouth.

Her hands clutched at the back of his neck and all semblance of control vanished. His groin hardened almost painfully. He clutched Lila's hips in his hands and held her closer to his lower body, feeling her move slightly. He thrust against her, sharpening the sensations in him.

He knew that Lila wasn't like the women he'd dated in the past, other executives from outside firms who were hardened by life and more cynical. No, Lila was different. She baked bread for the office when morale was low. She offered life, he realized, and though he knew he couldn't have it forever, he wanted a small slice of it for himself. He needed to believe for a few moments that he wasn't alone in the world.

Nick wanted to be a tender dream lover, but his body was on overdrive and he held on to his control by a string. His hands shook with the need to touch all of her. The low lighting in his office cast the room in a comforting glow. He loosened the buttons on her blouse, and met her clear gaze with his own.

No matter how badly he wanted this, he wasn't

going to push Lila to move too quickly. He didn't analyze why.

"Okay?" he asked, dipping one finger beneath her collar.

She nodded.

He released another button. Her skin was smooth and creamy, like the finest satin sheets. He leaned down to drop kisses on the flesh he'd exposed.

She shivered, her fingers tunneling in his hair and holding him close to her. He quickly opened the remaining buttons and stood back. Taking her wrists in his hands he held her arms away from her body. The bodice of her shirt fell open. A scrap of red satin and lace covered her breasts.

It enraged his senses the way nothing else ever had. It wasn't right that a bra meant for sin should be on her sweet body, but at the same time it was perfect. There was no other undergarment that could do this body justice.

He deftly opened the front closure of her bra. A quick intake of breath was her response. Deliberately, he bent and took the edge of the right cup between his teeth and slowly pulled the fabric away from her skin.

The stubble on his jaw scraped against her skin and she lifted her chest slightly. Her hands weren't as subtle, directing him to her nipple.

"Please," she said.

"Hell, yes."

He nibbled on her hardened flesh before suckling

her deep in his mouth. She held him tight to her body and blood engorged his sex, making him so hard and full he thought he'd explode before he moved on.

The slow pace he was trying to set evaporated. He took Lila's mouth as he planned to take her. Hard, swift but with infinite care, and he lifted her, carrying her to the cherrywood desk. He set her on its surface and slid his hands under her skirt.

He cursed when he found her warm, wet and wanting. Damn. He needed to fill her. To feel that humid heat on him. To revel in the fact that she wanted him as much as he wanted her.

His tongue thrust deeper into her mouth. Needing to deeply embed her essence on every one of his senses, he pulled her panty hose down over hips and legs. He wrenched his mouth from hers.

Urging her to lean back on the desk, support her own weight on her elbows, he spread her before him like a sensual feast. Her blouse fell away from her body exposing her flushed breasts with their hardened tips. Her skirt bunched at her waist revealing panties that matched her bra. His pulse jumped higher, and he couldn't breath until he'd tasted her intimately.

He sank back in his big leather chair and surrounded her hips with his hands. She glanced down at him, passion still in her eyes, but something else there, too.

"May I taste you?" he asked.

She nodded again.

He bent forward, resting his cheek against the lace

and satin that covered her mound. Then he slowly turned his face until he was surrounded by her scent. He couldn't wait any longer; standing, he ripped her panties from her body and carefully opened his fly.

Lila freed his long erection from his pants and brought him closer to her. The head of his manhood brushed against her and she moaned deep in her throat. She thrust against him, but Nick used his grip on her hips to slow the movement.

He slid carefully into her, slowly savoring each pulse around his hard length. She was small and tight, fitting him like a velvet glove. She tried to rush his possession, but he wouldn't let her. He was the master here. In her body he'd found the place where he should always be.

He seated himself to the hilt and paused for a moment.

"Keep going, Nick."

"Oh, I will," he said, but didn't move. Instead he bent to take her nipple into his mouth, sucking strongly until he felt her hips moving between his hands, felt the tiny tightening of her muscles against his manhood. Then he pulled out of her and started to thrust. Lila met him thrust for thrust, clutching his buttocks and pulling him to her.

The tension built inside him. He couldn't hold on another second, but he had to. He waited until he felt Lila's body clench around his, felt the extra warmth that hadn't been there before, and then let himself go.

Let his release take him to the stars and carry this sweet woman there with him.

He wanted to collapse against her but knew he couldn't, so he lifted himself away and sank back into his office chair. Eventually his pulse slowed and sanity returned. He zipped his pants and felt the stickiness of their joining. Damn, he hadn't used a condom.

Lila's descent to reality seemed to take a little longer, however. Nick knew the moment it happened because she grasped the edges of her blouse together and refused to look at him.

Some mistakes were the kind that took you years to realize, Lila thought as she fought to rebutton her silk blouse. And others stared you in the face from the moment the actions were taken. What had felt so right minutes earlier now felt horribly wrong.

Her heart ached and her stomach churned like a hurricane in the Atlantic. She tried to act calm but having had only one other lover in her life hadn't given her a lot of sophistication to call on in this type of situation. She slid off the desk and decided she could go home without panties or hose on because she sure as heck wasn't rooting around under his desk to find them.

With a calmness that she knew had to be some sort of protective shell, she smoothed her skirt, tucked her hair behind her ear and walked away from the man who'd just tilted her neat little world. First with the announcement that the safe predictable life she'd built at Colette was in danger, and then with the soul-searing intensity with which he'd made love to her.

Part of her thought the whole thing entirely romantic, but the forbidding look on Nick's face told her he wasn't going to get down on one knee and confess his undying devotion to her.

This heartache's on me, she thought, knowing that her fantasies about Nick had precipitated their love-making. She wanted to play it cool, but she was afraid if she tried to talk her voice would come out in a high-pitched squeak.

"Lila," Nick said. His voice was low and calm, washing over her like a warm breeze on a summer's day. She wanted to go to him and wallow in what he had to offer, but she knew it was a mirage.

"Yes," she said, picking up her laptop and preparing to leave, still refusing to look at him.

"We have to talk about what just happened."

Not if she lived to be a hundred would she ever want to discuss this with anyone. And certainly not with Nick. She made a noncommittal sound. Let him take that for whatever he wanted, she wasn't up for a post mortem right now.

She heard his footsteps and refused to glance at him. His body heat reached her in waves, and now that she knew how strong he was and how right it had felt to be in his arms, he was even harder to resist.

"Honey."

"Don't," she said, her voice cracking, as she'd feared it would. The way he'd pulled out of her body and sat in his chair waiting for her to recover told her more than words ever could. He did not think of her in an affectionate way, and she'd tolerate no lies from him.

"Lila, I didn't mean for any of this to happen but it did and nothing can change the fact that neither of us was prepared for it."

She became aware of the stickiness between her thighs. She knew immediately that he wasn't only concerned about health issues but about pregnancy. How careless could she be? she asked herself. Hadn't she learned anything growing up with her unmarried mother?

"I'm not on the pill," she said. She was one of the small percentage of women who were allergic to it. It had never bothered her because she wasn't swept away by desire. In fact, she had found the entire male-female lust-at-first-sight phenomenon to be highly overrated...until tonight.

"Well, hell," he said, then turned away from her to utter something profane and succinct.

His words cut straight to her heart.

"Yes, hell. This isn't the end of the world, you know." Chances were she wasn't pregnant.

Now he was the one avoiding eye contact. "It is for me."

"Why?" she asked.

"Because I made a vow never to marry again." His words affected her in a way she didn't want them to, and dashed her secret hopes once and for all. She'd been dreaming of Nick Camden for so long that she'd put him on a pedestal, and here he was revealing his very real clay feet.

"I don't recall asking you to marry me, Nick Camden."

His laser-sharp gaze pinned her to her spot. He didn't say anything in response to her sarcasm.

"If you're pregnant we can discuss the choices to be made."

"What are you insinuating, Nick?"

"That we will have to make some decisions once we know the full details of the situation."

"This sounds like the verbiage for a damned memo. This isn't about the job, you know. This is about life."

"My job *is* my life, Lila."

Truer words were never spoken.

"How soon until you'll know if you're knocked up?"

"Jeez, now that I've seen your charm I know why you're so popular with the ladies."

"Dammit, Lila—"

"Yes, dammit, Nick."

She walked out of his office and grabbed her purse from the bottom desk drawer.

"You didn't answer my question."

She sighed. She knew how dogged he could be when he set his mind to something. "A few days maybe. I'm not real regular."

She shut off her desk lamp and felt the heavy

weight of his hand on her shoulder. "I'll drive you home."

"No, thank you."

"It wasn't an offer."

"Was it an order?"

"Tell me you're not planning to walk home in the dark."

"I'm not planning to walk home in the dark," she said, feeling an edge that she normally tempered with lots of baking and a call to her mother.

"Smart-ass."

"Look, this is Youngsville, not Chicago. I'll be fine."

"You're not going without me and that's final."

"Okay," she said.

He grabbed his coat from the rack and reached around the corner to hit the light switch. Lila's discarded undergarments were under his desk. He stopped and pocketed them without a word. Then he closed and locked his inner office door. He took her elbow and escorted her down the darkened hallway.

Lila felt the emotions inside her swirling like a black mist and rising so quickly she couldn't control them. She knew she had to keep her mouth shut but somehow the words wouldn't stop.

"So I guess I shouldn't ask if it was good for you?"

Three

———

Nick had been at some low places in his life but never had he felt like this. The night was pitch dark and he was thankful that Lila was silent as they drove. He didn't think he could take much more conversation from her at this point. In his mind's eye he was surrounded by an image of Lila's wide brown eyes brimming with a sheen of tears.

Though his mind screamed for him to back away his body relived the incredible rightness that their joining had brought. And he knew that he should regret that he hadn't used a condom when they'd made love, but deep inside he was glad he hadn't. His groin still throbbed at the remembered feel of her around him.

Lila had been the fulfillment of his dreams, of what a woman could be. But she was his assistant, dammit. How could he have let this happen?

But he knew once hadn't been enough. In fact, as he came to a stop in front of her building, he knew that he wanted to come up tonight and mate with her again. To cement what was between them so that she didn't have to react with her sharp tongue.

"Well, thanks for the ride," she said and then a bitter laugh escaped her. "I meant the *car* ride."

"Lila, stop it. I'm sorry for the way that our first time happened, but I won't let you think it meant nothing to me."

"I'm sure you say that to all the girls, Nick."

"I don't have a stock of lines I pull out for the appropriate moment."

"I'm relieved."

She looked at him, but her expression was indiscernible in the feeble light of the street lamp. He knew his reaction earlier had made his comments seem, well, like a lie, but truer words had never been spoken. Lila meant more to him than the faceless ladies in his past and she deserved better than a burnt-out executive whose only emotion was cold, hard lust.

Except it hadn't felt cold or hard when he'd been with Lila. Buried in her sweet warm body he'd felt like he'd found the home he'd been forcing Colette, Inc. to be for years.

"Are you feeling better?"

She shook her head, the silky length of her blond

hair was illuminated by the light of the moon. He wished he'd taken his time with her. He wished they'd had all night to learn each other's bodies instead of a hurried explosion in his office. He wished that he could go back to the moment he'd pulled away from her and lie against her breast and comfort them both.

"I can't do this right now. I'm achy and not myself," she said.

"That's okay."

"No, it's not. I'm feeling mean, Nick. And I want to hurt you so deeply that you'll still feel it weeks from now."

"If it would make you feel better."

She looked out the window, and when she spoke again her voice was so soft he had to lean in to hear it. "My mother gave birth to me when she was only sixteen. I've never met my father."

Simple sentences. Simple words that summed up a life that was anything but simple. He hadn't realized how complex the situation was, but now he did.

"We're not in that situation."

"No?"

He wanted to do the right thing, to say he'd marry her if she found out she was pregnant with his child, but he knew he couldn't. The low points in his life were manageable because he'd found a way to guarantee they never happened a second time. He'd made the vow never to marry again because Amelia's death had cut through the layers of who he was and left him a quivering mound of insecurity. If there was one thing he wouldn't tolerate it was weakness.

"Well, you're not sixteen."

She reached for the door handle and Nick hit the locks.

"Let me out of the car."

"I can't."

"Don't be silly. You run a multimillion-dollar division for a large corporation, this should be a cinch for you."

"I want you to tell me that you'll stop beating yourself up about this. I seduced you."

"I had no idea you were this bossy in your personal relationships," she said, whipping her head around to face him. She leaned in close and he could taste her breath as it brushed across his face.

The leather seats and her scent teased his mind, tempted him to pull across the gearshift as he had this morning and kiss her until she was too exhausted to talk.

"You didn't seduce me."

He had. He knew he had. He'd been feeling out of control and had called on the one thing he could count on. Lila. She'd soothed him and comforted him and taken him out of his skin to a place he'd never really been before.

And he'd repaid her by possibly impregnating her. God, his technique could use some work. Except with Lila all those practiced moves didn't work.

"I'm not about to debate this with you. Thanks for bringing me home."

She manually unlocked the door and opened it. The chilly evening air swirled inside. It swept through the warmth and seeped into his clothing.

She closed the door and walked away without a backward glance. He watched the fluidity with which her limbs moved, while surrounded by the scent of her perfume and the chill of the autumn evening. The pain in his soul was unexpected but no less sharp than a knife to the gut.

Lila Maxwell already meant more to him than she should, but watching her walk away hurt. And knowing that he'd brought her pain added to the hurt that was layering through him.

Lila was tired by the time three o'clock rolled around. She'd been up since five in the morning baking pies and breads, which she'd dropped off at the Youngsville Nursing Home on her way to work. The route had taken her twenty minutes in the opposite direction, but she hadn't minded. She'd needed the therapy that baking had brought.

She'd tried leaving Rose's brooch at home but hadn't been able to. It complemented the deep-brown silk shirt she wore with a long black skirt.

Longingly, she fingered the piece of jewelry, then dropped her hands to her keyboard and forced herself to get back to work.

Nick had been out of the office all morning, which

meant she'd fielded a lot of calls from concerned staff on both the international and domestic teams. Lila didn't mind the extra time on the phone because it kept her mind busy. And busy meant away from that open door leading to Nick's office.

The phone rang as Nick returned to the office. Lila scheduled an appointment for Nick for the following week and pretended that he wasn't standing on the other side of her desk staring at her. Pretended that he was still just a casual acquaintance. Pretended that last night had never happened.

She concluded the call but didn't move. She was an efficient secretary until Nick walked into the room.

"Aren't you going to look at me?" he asked, taking the handset from her grip and depositing it in its cradle.

"Sure," she said, smiling up at him. All business, she reminded herself. "You need to sync your Palm Pilot. There are three urgent messages and an update to this afternoon's calendar."

"I'll do it right away. I'd like a few minutes of your time," he said. He was tired. He rubbed the back of his neck and loosened his tie. She wanted to pull him into her arms and offer him comfort. But couldn't.

She glanced at her day planner. Of course the afternoon was empty. But she wasn't ready to accommodate him. In the middle of the night as she lay in her bed staring at the cracks in the ceiling she'd realized that life gave you what you sought out. And she was seeking more than a man who couldn't commit to her.

"I'm in the middle of a proposal. Maybe later?" she suggested, knowing his afternoon was booked.

Suddenly she realized why people advised you not to get involved with someone at work. It made the atmosphere very tense and uncomfortable. Before, they'd been a team, and Lila had felt that she had his respect. But not anymore.

He put his hand on hers. It cut to the core. His big, warm hand surrounding her small one. Protecting, cherishing. His forefinger moving in a slow sweep from wrist to knuckles. "Lila..."

Not fair, she thought. But she nodded and stood, reluctantly tugging her hand from under his. "I only have five minutes."

"That's all I ask."

"I'll be right in." Lila waited until Nick left and forwarded her phone to one of the executive secretaries down the hall. The volume of calls today and the nature of them made her want to guarantee that someone answered the phone and reassured whoever called that Colette, Inc. was doing okay.

She entered Nick's office. Instead of seeing the plush surroundings she saw Nick sitting at his desk, looking a little lonely and very closed off. This was the man she'd hoped to reach.

"Have a seat."

She settled in his guest chair, trying hard to forget the incredible passion they'd shared on his cherrywood desk not even twenty-four hours ago, how his body had felt inside hers, how full and how right.

"I hope you're feeling better today."

"I wasn't ill yesterday," she said softly.

"I meant that smart mouth of yours."

"Oh." She wished she reacted to hurt the way others did, but she always lashed right back out. It was a holdover from her childhood, and she wished she could shake it but hadn't been able to yet.

"Well?" he asked.

"I'm fine."

"Good. I wanted to apologize for not protecting you."

She raised one eyebrow. "If you'd like me to keep my sarcasm hidden then please don't make any other comments like that."

"I didn't protect you, Lila."

"I'm just as much at fault. It wasn't as if we'd planned it. I'd have been surprised if you had pulled out a condom."

"I also wanted to reassure you that if there is a child, I'll offer you my full support."

Lila was surprised. "I thought you didn't want marriage."

"I meant financial and, of course, emotional support, but I won't marry again, especially not because of an unplanned pregnancy."

"Why not?"

Nick rubbed his eyes and stood, pacing to the window. "I was an unplanned child. My parents were forced to marry to give me legitimacy."

Lila's heart ached. She knew how it felt to know that your parents had conceived you by accident. But she'd also blossomed under the love of a mother who cherished her daughter and never allowed anyone to say that Lila was a mistake.

She walked over to Nick and slid her arm through his. She wanted to do so much more but didn't trust herself. "I came into the world the same way. My parents never married, though."

"Count yourself lucky. That kind of situation brings out the worst in people."

She wasn't sure what to say to that.

"I like you, Lila. You're funny, smart and sexy as hell. I don't want ever to wake up in the morning and see your face as my enemy."

His sincerity made her ache. She cupped her hand around his jaw, meeting his blue gaze squarely. "We're not our parents."

"I know. But we're already following in their footsteps."

"We don't have to."

"I'm not sure where we go from here."

Lila looked away. "We'll pretend it was a one-time thing. We can't make love again."

Both eyebrows rose, but he said nothing.

"You'll see. We'll get back into our groove here at work. Everything will work out."

"If you say so," he muttered.

"I do," she said and pivoted on her heel to leave.

"One more thing, Lila."

"Yes?"

"Let me know as soon as you've found out."

"I will." She walked away feeling as if she'd gone ten rounds with a title-fighter. But this was for the best. No matter how many nights she'd dreamt of Nick, she knew that he wasn't her reality man.

"Nick, do you have a minute?" Lila asked as Nick hung up the phone on a fruitless call to Grey Enterprises. He hadn't been able to get any information from the sales rep he'd been talking to. Maybe dinner and drinks would loosen the man's tongue.

Nick leaned back in his chair and glanced up at the woman responsible for making his life a living hell for the last two days. She treated him as a boss, and while he understood it was part of her plan, it wasn't helping.

Her red-and-black suit would have done justice to a power-monger on Wall Street, but on Lila it looked less threatening. He knew that she prided herself on her professional image and wondered how much of that attitude had to do with her wanting their relationship back on a business-only level.

If anything, her behavior had sharpened the desire coursing through his veins. Watching her try to keep her distance made him want to bridge the gap. He had the urge to needle her out of her work mode and make her react to him as a man, not as her superior.

Work usually consumed all of his waking hours. But lately, at the oddest moments, the image of Lila, her weight braced on her elbows and her skirt around her hips, would enter his mind. He'd gotten an erection in a staff meeting yesterday afternoon. Never had any woman interfered with his job.

"What do you need?" he asked, to get his mind off her tempting curves.

She entered his office, moving with the subtle grace of a confident lady. "It's about the annual charity event."

Every year Colette, Inc. sponsored a bachelorette auction that featured the new fall and winter jewelry designs. Calling on single women from Colette's many departments to be auctioned off for dates, they had the evening gowns donated from a local designer and then each woman wore a signature piece of jewelry that would be for sale during the Christmas season.

The money raised from the auction went to a local children's home and the event was a big community satisfier for Colette. Nick had even bid on one of the bachelorettes last year.

"What about it?" he asked. The administrative staff each handled different aspects of the event.

"Is it still on? I've been getting a few calls about it. And it's already October."

"Nothing has changed at Colette. We want the public to see that we're still strong. It's definitely on." The more Nick thought about, he knew they'd have to do an intensive marketing campaign in Youngsville and the surrounding areas. The community needed to believe that Colette wasn't taking the Grey threat lying down.

"Good. I'll get the ball rolling on the planning."

She stood to leave his office, and he knew he couldn't endure another day of pretending he'd never been more to her than the man who employed her. "Lila, would you like to join me for lunch?"

She tilted her head to the side. Her eyes said yes but from past experience he knew how carefully she weighed every decision she made. It still surprised him she'd made love to him that night in his office.

Unless she'd been thinking about it for a while. But he wasn't going to ask her that. Then he'd sound like some dopey guy who'd never had incredible sex before. And he'd had plenty of incredible sex. Lots of it. But never as good as it had been with Lila.

"I don't think that would be a good idea," Lila said.

He knew he should let it go. Let *her* go. But he couldn't. "Why not?"

She bit her lip and glanced over her shoulder at the open doorway leading to her desk. "I don't want people getting the wrong idea about us, especially since we agreed our business relationship is what's important."

A blush flooded her face and neck. He wondered where it started. At her pert breasts? Or higher? Did the warmth flooding her skin also affect other more intimate parts of her body?

"You're my secretary, no one would think there was anything else involved," he said.

"I don't know. You look at me sometimes in a way that's just not…"

She was too perceptive, he thought. He did look at her like he didn't know what to do with her. And he didn't. She'd managed to get under his skin and he couldn't decide how to get her out.

"We'll talk about the auction."

"I don't think so. I don't want to take a chance."

"A chance on what?"

She said nothing. He hated her silences. Hated that he knew he wouldn't be able to keep quiet because anger grew inside him. Hated that she was so calm and cool while he simmered with frustration.

"A chance that someone might think that we close the door sometimes late at night and make love on my desk?" he asked.

She glanced away. He knew he'd hurt her with his words, and he wanted to call them back. He was a bastard. He knew better than to talk to anyone when he felt this way. And it wasn't as if the situation with Lila was her fault.

"Not sometimes," she said, striding out of his office. She pulled his door toward her and before it closed, she said, "One time."

Nick picked up the crystal paperweight he'd been given when he'd gotten his first promotion at Colette and heaved it at the wall. Then he grabbed his coat and left his office, not glancing once at the woman who'd caused a roar inside him that couldn't be silenced with social niceties and childish games of do-overs.

He continued down the hall and took the stairs, fifteen damned flights of stairs outside to the fresh sunshine. Except that the darkness inside him threatened to black out the sunshine. His carefully controlled life had spun out of control and as it started to settle, none of the pieces fell where they belonged.

Four

Lila left her desk after Nick's departure. She knew Nick wasn't comfortable with their new relationship, but she was afraid to let her emotions get involved with Nick.

Suddenly she realized they already were. Even if she never touched him again, even if physically they lived in other parts of the world, he'd always be a part of her. If she never saw him again, he'd still haunt her dreams, not only as a phantom lover but as a man she cared about.

The sun shone brightly on this early October day. It was chilly outside and her suit, though lined and long-sleeved, was no match for the wind. If she ever moved again it would be back to someplace warm. Hawaii warm.

She scanned the parking lot looking for his car and saw him striding toward the park across the street. She didn't hesitate to follow him. But once he sat on a bench she was reluctant to approach. She had no idea what to say.

"Stop hovering, Maxwell."

She sighed, lowering herself to the wooden bench. She glanced around to make sure no one saw her sitting with Nick, but the lunch crowd was light at the moment.

"Why'd you follow me?" he asked.

"I wanted to clear up a few things." Darn, it was really cold by the lake. A stiff breeze ruffled her hair and she tried to tuck the escaping strands back into her chignon. She hugged her arms around her waist.

"Yes?"

"It's not you I don't want to be seen with."

"Yeah, right," he said.

"It's just I have a solid reputation here. You've probably always had one, having grown up in an intact family. But for me, everyone always said, like mother, like daughter."

"Are you like your mother?" he asked.

"Until two nights ago, no."

"Our intimacy changed that?" He shrugged out of his suit jacket and then draped it over her shoulders. She huddled into it. Still warm from his body, it was like being enveloped in Nick. She wanted that again. Not just the passion but the cuddling they'd missed out on.

"Yes. Mom was always..."

"Your mom's promiscuous?"

"No. She just doesn't care what others think. She lives by her own rules."

"Then what was the problem?"

"Honestly, Nick, look at me. I don't know why but I don't make friends easily."

"I think you should take your mother's attitude."

"That's easy for you to say. I've created a nice life for myself in Youngsville. People respect me and I'm a part of the community. I don't want to lose that."

He glanced away out over the lake. She wondered what he saw there. Wondered if it brought him peace of mind. She'd seen him at this bench a handful of times since she started working for him. It was where he cleared his mind.

She also knew that this bench was visible from all of the window offices. Subconsciously it seemed she'd made up her mind even if she didn't want to admit it. She wasn't going to let Nick slip away. She was going to have to face her fears. Was he worth the risk?

"I don't think you'll be ostracized for eating lunch with me."

She stared into his electric-blue eyes and knew she could easily lose herself in them. "You want more than lunch, don't you?"

"So do you," he said softly. He was right, she did want more. More than he had offered her. She wondered if she could settle for halfway.

She didn't say anything. His words went through her like a carnal kiss. Her pulse sped up and her breasts felt tight. A warmth penetrated her and forced her to admit the truth. An uncomfortable truth she hadn't been prepared for.

"Listen, we're under enough pressure at work with the takeover attempt. Why don't we try again?"

Lila wanted to say yes without thinking but that would be a mistake. "I'm not looking for a red-hot affair."

"That's all I have to offer, Lila."

"You have more, you just aren't interested in the wholesome, all-American family with me."

"No. I've just seen what marriage can do."

"I know," she said. "Face of the enemy and all that."

"Don't scoff. You're more concerned with other's opinions than you are with anything else."

"Maybe we both need to change a little," she admitted.

"I don't know if I want to."

"Our world is changing."

"One date? We might decide we don't like each other," he cajoled.

"Do you have a nasty habit you've been hiding from me?"

"Probably more than one. Will you have dinner with me tomorrow?"

"I have tickets to the symphony. They're doing an evening of Gershwin." She'd never been to concerts, theatre or the ballet as a child. But her mother had made her watch a lot of "Great Performances" on PBS and every Sunday they'd listen to classical music or opera after church. It had given her an appreciation for different types of music that many of her peers didn't have.

She loved that she could afford to hold season tickets to the symphony. Usually she invited Mrs. Tooney or Mrs. Appleton from the seniors' center. They were always looking for something to do outside the center. Or she took one of her friends from Amber Court.

"I'll take you to dinner first," Nick said.

"A lot of people from Colette will be at the symphony," she said.

"It's your call."

No guts, no glory, she thought. This was her chance to see if Nick Camden really was the man for her. "Yes, I'll go."

"Come on, let's get back to the office before you freeze to death."

Nick teased her all the way back to the building about the weather and her thin blood. The imprint of his hand on her lower back lingered long after he'd gone into his office and she'd called Meredith, her friend and co-worker, to talk about the details of the charity auction.

The next evening, Nick questioned his reasons for asking Lila out for a date. He knew nothing could come of it. Knew that he'd give anything for one full night in her bed. Knew that he wanted more with her than he'd had for a long time with anybody.

He'd made a reservation at Crystal's for the evening. The posh restaurant with its fireplaces and French food was the perfect place for seduction. In fact, he'd taken many women there before. He hadn't realized that until he'd exchanged looks with the maître d'. Pierre had seated him with many different women and it tainted the evening for Nick.

Lila seemed oblivious as she took her seat. They were close enough to the fire to feel its heat. Nick had never been nervous about a date before so at first he didn't recognize the symptoms. He'd graduated from high school when he was sixteen and started college early. He'd wanted to escape his parents so badly that he put everything else on hold. So sweaty palms weren't the norm for him.

Most of the women he'd dated had pursued him before he'd asked them out, so they'd eagerly accepted. Not Lila. She'd thought twice about the evening, had even doubled-checked with him before leaving the office to make sure he hadn't changed his mind.

Her question had roused a tenderness in him that he was unfamiliar with. He hadn't been able to shake it as he'd dressed and driven to her apartment. When she'd opened her apartment door, the tenderness had changed to lust. Not totally changed, as he would have liked, but lust was now the overriding emotion.

Dammit, it wasn't fair that she looked like an angel

and carnal sin at the same time. He didn't know how to handle her. In fact, she was the only thing in his life that had thrown him for a loop in a long time. Even the takeover attempt which was rocking his world didn't affect him the way Lila did. He knew he could find another job. Sure it would be a struggle, but so had his entire life. Lila offered a different view and he had no idea how to handle her.

Her sweater was pink and soft, hugging the curves of her breasts and making her skin glow. She wore pearl-gray trousers and tasseled loafers. It was the first time he'd seen her in something other than a business suit—or partially naked. These casual clothes showed him a glimpse of the woman Lila hid under her professional veneer. She had on an exquisite amber-and-precious-metal brooch. It was unusual for him not to recognize the designer. Having worked his way up in sales, he knew not only the "signatures" of the Colette designers but of most other designers in their field.

"Where'd you get that brooch?"

"Oh, Rose lent it to me."

"Who's Rose?"

"My landlady. It's so silly, but she said it always brought love to those who wore it."

Hell. "Are you looking for love, Lila?"

"I'm not searching for it, but if I find it I'm not going to run away."

"Well, I guess that piece is as good a talisman as any."

"Don't you believe in love, Nick?"

He shook his head. He wasn't ready to get into a discussion on what he'd seen done in the name of love. He knew for a fact that it didn't exist. Had never felt any great melting in his heart when he'd met his wife or thought of his deceased parents.

"I wonder who designed the piece?"

"I could ask Rose."

"Don't bother. I was just curious."

The waiter arrived and they both ordered. The sommelier stopped by next.

"Would you like a glass of wine with dinner?"

Lila nodded. Nick selected a French burgundy. One of the benefits of traveling in Europe was that he'd learned the difference between a gallon of grocery bargain wine and the French and Californian vineyards.

An awkward silence fell between them. Lila straightened her silverware and then glanced up at him. She blushed when she caught him staring at her.

"The atmosphere at work is getting pretty hairy," she said.

Nick grunted. The situation with Grey was getting worse. Rumors ran out of control like weeds in a garden and there was little the executive committee could do but smile and lie through their collective teeth. Nick usually felt calm at work. He knew the entire staff all worked hard and the company was solvent. This takeover attempt involved more than money, his gut said.

"What's the word?" he asked her.

"Rumors of unfair business practices. I couldn't run it down though. Even Paula in Human Resources was tight-lipped."

"A miracle has occurred somewhere if Paula was tight-lipped."

"No doubt. Maybe the second coming."

Tonight, though, he wanted to put thoughts of Colette on hold and focus on Lila. On him and Lila—together.

"Well, enough about work. Tell me about yourself, Lila."

"Why?"

"Because I'm interested in getting to know you."

"Pretty much what you see is what you get," she said, softly.

"I know there's more."

"What else do you know?"

"I know that your temper gets the best of you sometimes and you say things you normally wouldn't. I know that you bake when you are scared and that's probably why everyone on our floor took home a basket of cookies this afternoon."

"Is that all?" she asked, leaning forward. Her sweater hugged the curves of her cleavage. Nick stared at the creamy globes of her breasts and remembered the feel of her nipple in his mouth. Remembered the way it had hardened as he'd suckled. His mouth watered.

"I also know the sound you make when I'm buried

deep inside you. And I'd give ten years off my life to hear that sound again.''

Lila could think of nothing but Nick's words to her in the restaurant. For once the music of Gershwin didn't sweep into her soul and take her away from her mundane life. For once the thought of her peers seeing her out with her boss didn't bother her. For once she could only focus on the man next to her and whether she'd invite him in when they got home.

His voice, low and husky, brushed over her senses as he leaned closer and whispered something in her ear. She couldn't make out the words. His scent surrounded her and she closed her eyes for a moment, wanting this night to live forever in her memory.

She'd never flown by emotion before. Never given in to the urges that were now sweeping through her. The same urges that had led her to make love with him on his desk.

Wake up, Lila.

But she knew she wasn't dreaming. He was at once better than she'd dreamed he'd be and at the same time worse. Better because reality was warm skin and electric tingles, soft whispers and light, teasing kisses. Worse because he wasn't interested in the long-term the way she'd dreamed he would be. The way she needed him to be if she were pregnant with his child.

The orchestra played ''Someone to Watch Over Me.'' Lila felt the tears sting the backs of her eyes. She was transported back to her girlhood living room, to the battered Salvation Army couch and faded orange shag rug. Her mother holding her close and singing that bittersweet song along with an old Lena Horne recording. Her mother's voice wept with a longing that had always made Lila want to hide from the night.

Tonight the words seemed a warning, a reminder that love is blind. That what she felt for Nick was more like blind lust than love. She was throwing away her reputation for a man who was only looking for what she could give him in the darkest hours of the night.

Oh, God.

She searched through her purse for a tissue and found a snowy white handkerchief being handed to her instead. She felt trapped, like a vinyl record that had a skip in it and kept playing the same few bars of a song.

Was she doomed to be the same woman her mother was? She didn't look at Nick, just nodded her thanks and wiped her eyes. Exposed and vulnerable, she turned away from him and forced herself to the present.

The house lights came up and everyone filed out of the auditorium. But Lila didn't move. Her mind and body still hummed with the music she'd just heard. And, though it had brought her to tears, it had also enervated her body.

Also, she was honest enough to admit, she wasn't ready to get into that car again with Nick. His intimate, leather-smelling sports car that made her think of hot sex and steamy winter nights.

"Ready?" he asked at last. Most of the audience was gone by this time and Lila knew she was inviting the speculation that she'd always avoided.

"Yes." She started to hand back his handkerchief but decided she should probably wash it first. She slid it into her purse and followed him out into the night.

A harvest moon lit the evening sky and few stars could be seen in its bright glare. The air was cool and crisp but not unpleasantly so as Lila put her head back and looked up at the stars. She realized how small she was in the world.

She touched her stomach thinking of the child that could possibly be inside her. Nick's hand rested on top of hers. She looked up into his eyes and saw that something had changed since they'd entered the theater. She didn't understand it but there was no longer just lust in his eyes. Now there was something that looked more permanent. But Lila didn't trust herself enough to pursue it.

"I want to promise to watch over you," he said, so softly she barely caught the words. His earnest longing closed the back of her throat.

"But you can't," she said.

He pulled her close to him, holding her against that broad, strong chest of his that could protect her from any earthly threat, but not from the one thing that would hurt the most. Nick Camden.

Nick clasped her hand in his. "Let's walk down by the lake. There's a nice view."

Too tired and drained from the evening of Gershwin and feeling like she was in a fish bowl, Lila let him get away with changing the subject. "Really?"

"Yes. And a comfortable bench."

Trying for a lightness she didn't feel, she said, "You know, in Florida we have lakes all over the place. But Lake Michigan…it's so grand."

He smiled at her. "I learned to ski on that lake."

He never talked of his childhood, she realized. Except for that moment when he'd mentioned the war zone that his parents' marriage had been. "Who taught you?"

They walked in the dappled light provided by the trees. "Buster McKee's dad."

"Was Buster your friend?"

"Kind of. His dad was really great."

"Why?" she asked.

"He always had time for me. I mean I was a stubborn kid. I'd decided early on that I was the only one I could depend on."

"But he took the time for you?"

"Yeah, he did." Nick brushed his fingers through her hair and turned her face to his.

His eyes were half-closed, and she couldn't read anything in his gaze, but she wanted to. She wanted to know what he was feeling. To ascertain she wasn't the only one out of control.

"I'm going to kiss you."

She leaned closer and stood on her tiptoes.

"I take it you don't mind."

She smiled up at him. A kiss was just what she needed to end this evening. Because she knew that she wasn't going to ever have the opportunity to date Nick Camden again. She'd made a mistake thinking they could forget about that incredible sexual encounter they'd had. Made a mistake thinking that they could just continue on their merry way as if the world hadn't changed.

Because it had and it would never be the same between them again.

She kissed him. But in her heart she knew it was goodbye.

Five

Ah, hell, Nick thought. Lila's mouth under his was the sweetest fruit he'd ever tasted. Brushing his lips back and forth over hers only, he teased the both of them.

Hot breath was exchanged, and Nick swore to himself as he felt himself harden. Lila's hands held his head, as though she'd never let him go. He put his thoughts on hold and let his hormones take control.

Nick deepened the kiss. The inside of her mouth was warm and welcoming the way her body had been when they'd made love. He wanted to make love to her again. That night had been the last sane moment in his life. And it had been so far from normal that it shouldn't have been.

He thrust his tongue deep inside her and for the moment tried to quench a thirst that couldn't be quenched. Her tongue brushed against his, not shyly but like that of a woman who knew what she wanted. And what she wanted was within her grasp.

Nick slid his hands inside her coat and down her back, cupping her behind. He pulled her closer to his aching body. She moaned deep in her throat. Damn, he'd started something he couldn't finish here.

He wished they were at his place, on his big king-size bed where he could spread Lila out and take his time loving her. Because that was what they both needed. Especially him.

A cool breeze blew across the lake. Lila shivered in his arms and he pulled her closer. Lifting his mouth from hers he pushed her head against his chest and looked out over the vast expanse of water. It was a cold, lonely night, and having Lila in his arms should have assuaged those feelings, but it didn't. It sharpened them. He felt much the same as he had in his early twenties when he'd married Amelia and then learned she was sick. He'd had a glimpse of something he'd always longed for and then it was snatched away.

It wasn't that he was a cynic, he thought. He was a realist. He was meant to live alone.

Alone, he repeated to himself.

Why then did this one woman feel so right in his arms? Why then did her scent seem embedded in his soul? Why then did his body only feel alive when she was pressed intimately to him?

He breathed through his mouth, preparing to let go of her. *For good.*

"Let's get you home, Florida girl," he said, his voice sounding raspy to his own ears.

His erection still throbbed and for a minute he tried to figure out a way to make love in his two-seater sports car. The logistics wouldn't be bad if he was still a teenager, but he was a grown man. A responsible man...a horny man.

Damn.

"Mine or yours?" she asked.

Unable to believe she'd said the words he'd wanted to hear, it took a moment to respond. As much as he longed to spend the night in her bed he knew he couldn't. He wasn't the type of guy who carried condoms around. Though he'd dated a lot, he preferred planned seduction. But with Lila, there was no thought involved. Maybe he should start. He gave a harsh laugh, wishing for a moment that he could stop letting a certain part of his anatomy do his thinking.

"Yours, and then I'll go home to mine."

"Why? Despite my reaction to the song, Nick, I don't want you to watch over me. I'm a big girl, I can make my own decisions."

"I wasn't trying to watch over you."

"Yes, you were."

"The last time I stuck my tongue in your mouth

we made love on my desk, Lila. Give me a little credit for trying to do the right thing."

"A little credit, that's all you want?"

"Hell, no. I want you on my bed, spread in front of me like a feast so that I don't have to rush. I want to savor every inch of you."

"Then come home with me," she said.

He'd never had a harder time saying no. He shook his head.

"Face of the enemy and all that. Give me a break, Nick. This has to mean more than physical pleasure."

He hated that she kept throwing those words back at him. Especially when he was doing the noble thing here.

"Nah, I'm just—" looking to get laid, but he couldn't say that to her. Because he was afraid she'd hear the truth behind the words. What he really was, was needy. And she was the one thing he needed.

"Just what?"

Why couldn't she leave well enough alone?

"Nick?"

"Cut me some slack here, Lila."

"I wish it were that simple. But you make me feel things so extremely that I can't help myself."

"What can't you help?"

"Wanting you to be as vulnerable as I am."

"What makes you think I'm not?"

"All you want from me is sex."

"I wouldn't have stopped if that were true."

"Dammit, Nick. What *do* you want from me?"

"I don't know." He wished he could say all he wanted was a night of their hot bodies writhing on his bed. That was something he could label and feel safely. But the emotions that Lila brought to the surface were neither safe nor easily labeled.

She said nothing. Just wrapped her own arms around her waist, protecting herself from the hurt he seemed to wield like a sword. It proved what he'd known all along. He brought destruction to those who cared for him. First his parents' marriage, then Amelia's life. He wasn't about to add Lila to the list.

Mrs. Charlotte Tooney had married her childhood sweetheart and spent twenty happy years with him until one day he'd had a heart attack at work, leaving her alone for the first time in her life. She had original artwork on the walls of her apartment and an electric organ on which she sometimes played Al Martino songs.

Lila admired the woman's resilience in the face of the fact that she'd spent the last twenty years essentially alone. She had no children but had a happy, fulfilled life. Lila wanted that.

But at the same time she'd put off taking a pregnancy test so that she wouldn't have to confront the fact that she might not be pregnant with Nick's child.

"Did you try that recipe I gave you for jalapeño bread?" Charlotte asked, interrupting Lila's thought.

Charlotte spent a lot of time watching TV cooking shows and jotting down recipes for Lila to try. And honestly, most of them were good. "Not yet. It was a cookie night last night."

The small apartments for the elderly at the nursing house shared an open common area. Lila had met Charlotte and her best friend, Myrtle, her first week in Indiana when she'd brought books to donate to the home's small library and had struck up a conversation with the two women.

To Lila, Charlotte and Myrtle were the grandmothers she'd never had.

"Tell me about Gershwin. Did you take Myrtle with you?" Charlotte asked.

"No, she didn't," said Myrtle Frye, who had entered the apartment without knocking.

"Who'd you take?" Charlotte asked.

"Charlotte, that's none of our business."

"Yes, it is. Was it a man?"

"Yes. But it's not what you think," Lila said. Unless what you're thinking is that I made mad, passionate love with him that one night and then found out the last thing he wants in his life is a wife and child.

"The concert was good. I had a nice time." Lila glanced at the cuckoo clock on the wall. "I've got to get going. Enjoy the cookies."

"We will, sweetie."

"Are you taking some to that man?" Myrtle asked.

"What man?"

"The one who got to go to our concert," Charlotte said.

"No," she said. She wasn't sure what to do about Nick, but she knew that bringing him cookies wasn't the right thing. She'd been thinking more about their relationship as she'd baked. He'd seemed so raw in the Colette, Inc. parking lot. Not in command the way he usually was.

She put on her coat and headed for the door. "Bye, ladies."

"Bye, Lila."

There was a bus stop at the bottom of the hill. Though Lila had driven her car from Florida to Indiana when she'd moved, she hardly ever used it. Especially not in the fall and winter. She really hated driving.

Standing in the sun, waiting for the bus, she realized two things. If she was pregnant, she wanted to share the upbringing of that child with a spouse. And the only person she could picture as her spouse was Nick. So that meant she'd have to hold her temper and convince him that love existed. That the face on the pillow next to his in the morning wasn't an enemy's but an ally's.

But how?

Before she could do that she needed to face the truth herself. She needed to get a pregnancy test and see if she was going to be a mom.

"Lila?"

She turned to see Nick standing behind her. He wore a pair of tight faded jeans and a cable-knit sweater that should have made him look like any other man on a Saturday. But he didn't. He looked big and strong and like the man whose voice had just made her heart skip a beat.

"What are you doing here?"

"Visiting Mr. McKee."

"The guy who taught you to water-ski?" she asked.

"Yeah, Buster lives in Hawaii."

"That's nice." It was something she'd never have suspected Nick of doing. He was solitary by nature. He kept boundaries between himself and those around him. Mr. McKee must have had a deep impact on his life.

It made her realize what kind of father he'd be. Because the type of person who'd spend a Saturday with the elderly was the kind of guy who could make a commitment.

He shrugged. "What were you doing?"

"Dropping off some cookies," she said.

"You want a ride home?"

She wanted to spend more time with him. The high energy he usually radiated was tuned down. "Um, I don't want to take you out of your way."

"I'm going in to the office. So I'll have to go right by your place."

"I have an errand to run. You better just go on."

"I'll take you wherever you need to go."

She glanced across the yard at him. The bus should be here any minute. "I was going to the drugstore."

"Condoms?" he said, almost teasingly.

Maybe it would be better to let him believe that. But once you started talking in half truths it was so hard to go back to honesty. "No, pregnancy test."

He thrust his hands in his pockets. "Can you take one this soon?"

Less than a week, she thought. Was it too early to tell? "I don't know. I was going to check and see."

"I'll go with you," he said.

"It might be weird." Especially if they saw someone from the office. She could conceivably explain going to the symphony with Nick but shopping for pregnancy test kits together was not something she wanted to talk about to her co-workers.

"I can live with it."

This was it, she thought. If she wanted to teach Nick about love and commitment she had to start here. "Okay."

He walked back up the hill as the bus approached and Lila followed him. The Porsche was warm from the sun and, as she slid into it, she realized that she could get used to this; get used to spending lazy Saturdays with Nick. And that idea comforted her deep in her heart.

Seeing Mr. McKee always brought back bittersweet memories of his childhood. Long, hot afternoons spent skiing and boating on Lake Michigan. The longing for the family that Buster had and that Nick never would.

He'd tried it once with his own family. He'd taken

three months of saved allowances when he was four-teen and rented a boat and skis for the afternoon. His father and mother hadn't spoken to each other the entire time they were on the lake. It wasn't what he'd been trying to find, and it had strengthened Nick's desire to leave Youngsville behind.

It reminded him as well that he'd promised to be the kind of father that Mr. McKee had been, not the kind Guy Camden had. Involved in his son's life, not removed. The kind of guy who'd coach Little League baseball and teach his own flesh and blood how to water-ski in the summer.

Nick realized that he didn't have the lifestyle that would enable him to be an involved dad. He was a total workaholic more concerned with his job than with anything else. His work was, quite simply, his life. He couldn't imagine it any other way.

Following Lila down an aisle in the pharmacy to procure a test kit seemed like the right thing to do. He knew marriage wasn't an option. Or was it? He'd tried it once and the decision never to remarry wasn't one he'd made easily.

Lila and this possible baby made him want to dream again. Dreams he'd had as a boy. Before life had shaped him into the man he'd become. But that man knew those dreams would never come true.

He needed time away from Lila to decide. He knew he wasn't going to be uninvolved in his child's life if there was a child, but a wife....

Lila stopped, glanced both ways and pulled a box

from the shelf, skimming the back quickly before once again checking the aisle for other customers. Though it sometimes annoyed him, her preoccupation with what others thought was kind of endearing.

She looked cute today wearing a pair of navy leggings and a bright-colored sweater. She had on a winter coat that was a little heavy for the fall weather, but he knew she was cold most of the time. For someone who'd chosen to move north she seemed ill prepared for it.

"I could stand watch at that end," he said.

"Ha-ha. This isn't like the symphony. I think that we should know definitely before we have to deal with any rumors," she said.

She looked so cute, though, the way she kept glancing over her shoulders, that he wanted to kiss her. But he couldn't. Not here, not now.

He watched her and thought of the night they'd made love on his desk. Thought of all the things he'd do differently the next time he had her in his arms. And he'd definitely make love to her again.

"Did you find one?" he asked, ready to leave the drugstore. Maybe she'd let him kiss her before she got out of his car. In fact, he wasn't going to wait for her permission to do so. He was just going to kiss her.

"I think so. But most of these aren't good until I've missed a period." Her full lips beckoned him. She'd used some red lipstick earlier and only a trace remained. He wanted to remove the rest of it.

"Have you?" He didn't think she had because, most likely she would have mentioned it. And besides, it had only been six days. Not that he was counting.

"Not yet, but I should know soon."

"Why don't we wait?" he asked. He couldn't believe those words had come from his lips. He dealt in reality, but for a few days he wouldn't mind living in the realm of maybe.

"Don't you want to know?" she asked. Her face was lined with worry, and it brought home again how he'd failed to protect her. Dammit, when was he going to stop hurting those around him?

He hugged her close. He couldn't help it. She was so tiny compared to him. Her bones were small and fragile under his arms and he nestled her close to his body. Surrounded her with himself and promised not to hurt her again. "Sure, but not knowing for a few more days isn't going to change anything."

She slipped out of his embrace. "I'm going to buy this one, so I'll have it on hand."

He followed her down the aisle towards the registers, plowing into her when she came to an abrupt stop.

"Oh, God. That's my landlady, Rose. I don't want her to see me buying this."

"Calm down, Lila. You go talk to her, and I'll buy the kit."

"What if she saw us together? What if she knows what we're purchasing?"

"It's not like she's going to make you wear a scarlet A."

"This is serious. Your reputation can be stained by the smallest innuendo."

"Florida girl, you worry too much. She's coming this way, so smile." Nick took the package from her hand and strode toward the drug counter at the back of the store. He'd pay for the damn thing there.

He couldn't help thinking that Lila was never going to want to have a child without a husband. It bothered him, because the opinions of others were so fickle, but her anxiety was genuine and he didn't want to be the cause of more.

He knew he should transfer her out of his department. Except, with all the turmoil at Colette, that would just cause rumors to spread. And he didn't want anyone else sitting at the desk outside his office. It didn't matter that right now they didn't have the smoothest working relationship. Lila was his. And he wasn't letting her go.

He didn't examine that desire too closely. Just paid for the damn pregnancy kit and asked for a brown bag. Lila's landlady eyed the bag when Nick returned, and he knew she thought he'd purchased condoms. He felt a faint blush steal over his face as the older lady winked at him.

He wasn't ready to be part of a community, and he suddenly realized that was one of the things that scared him about Lila. She had woven herself into the fabric that was Youngsville, and he'd never wanted to be any part of it.

Six

Two days later, Lila was back at the office and still not sure where she stood with Nick. Saturday had been a strange glimpse into his personal life, and she couldn't happily blend it with what she already knew of him.

He was calm, self-assured and focused on work. But the other man was very real. More faceted than the one-dimensional image she'd carried of Nick. It was the picture of a man who'd been hurt and whose life had been shaped by those pains.

She realized she wanted to influence the direction his life took. She'd spent half the night lying in the dark staring at the stars she'd painted on her ceiling and had realized that she didn't want Nick in her personal life only if she was pregnant with his child. She wanted him to be with her always, but he didn't believe he deserved happiness.

Even though he'd never said those words, she knew that he believed he deserved to be punished. Something about the way he'd focused solely on his career after his wife's death. Something about the types of women he dated. Something about his reaction to her and the possibility of her pregnancy.

She picked at the salad she'd brought for lunch. Nick had been in back-to-back meetings all day, and she'd heard more than one rumor about the takeover. To be honest, she was worried that her time at Colette, Inc. was running short.

"Working through lunch?" Nick asked as he entered the office.

"Yes. I wanted to be here when you got back. There's an emergency board meeting scheduled for this evening. They want to look at last year's numbers compared to this year's."

"Have you contacted Jill in our business office?"

"Yes. They're running the numbers now. Jill is meeting with you at 3:30. That gives you a half hour to get her information and assimilate it."

"Great."

"Did you eat at your meeting?" she asked. She normally didn't like to run out and get lunch. She felt it put secretaries back to the dark ages if they offered to bring food or coffee for their boss.

But Nick looked tired. Was he having a hard time

sleeping through the night? Did worry about her or Colette keep him awake?

She hoped it was Colette, but at the same time feared it might be her. Their relationship was like a hurricane: stormy and out of control. They seemed to be in the eye right now. Everything calm and smooth, but still a tension underlay all their interactions.

"I'll grab a sandwich in the cafeteria."

"Before you go down there…"

"Yes?"

"I've heard some rumors you might want to be prepared for."

He took a deep breath.

"Nick, let me get you something, okay?"

"Okay. Tuna on wheat."

"I'll be right back."

Lila hurried to the cafeteria and got Nick's sandwich, avoiding most of her co-workers by keeping her head down and taking the stairs. Nick was seated behind his desk and was on the phone when she returned.

He hung up when she came in. She handed him his sandwich. "Close the door and come in for a minute."

His serious expression worried her. "Is this another bad-news scenario?"

"No. I'd like you to tell me what those rumors concern."

Lila was used to being Nick's ears around the

building, but this rumor involved one of Nick's best managers. "Unfair hiring practices."

"Am I supposed to be involved?" he asked.

She shook her head. "I haven't heard your name, but Paul was mentioned."

"Damn."

"That's what I thought you'd say."

"Get me fifteen minutes with Paul and Human Resources."

"I've got them down at 2:30. That gives you about twenty minutes to scarf down your sandwich."

"Do you need anything else?"

"One more thing."

Lila moved closer to Nick's desk, prepared to grab a sheet of paper and jot down whatever he wanted her to do. But Nick stood up and leaned forward, his face inches from hers.

"I need something from you, Lila."

"What?" she asked, her voice a husky whisper.

His breath brushed across her face and she closed her eyes, enjoying the sensation, remembering the last time they'd kissed. It seemed like forever since they'd touched.

The moist brush of his tongue across the seam of her lips surprised her. She opened her eyes and met his sensual gaze. He rubbed his lips back and forth on hers.

"Will you let me kiss you?" he asked.

Her first impulse was to crawl over his desk and pull him into her arms, but she didn't. Bracing her weight on her hands, she leaned farther over. Tilting her head to one side, she licked her lips.

His eyes tracked the movement. "Don't tease me, woman."

"I'm not."

"Yes, you are. And all I can think of when you are in my office is that night when I took you on my desk."

"Mc, too."

"Hell, Lila. Don't tell me that."

"Why not?"

"Because hearing you remember it too makes me want to take you again."

"Here?"

"No, not here."

"Then kiss me, Nick. And make it count."

Nick loosened his tie as he headed into the darkened parking lot toward his Porsche. He needed something to relieve the tension that had been riding him all afternoon. The meetings had not gone well.

All he'd been able to think of was Lila's sweet mouth as she'd kissed him with a carnality that had made his mind turn to mush and his loins painfully hard. He couldn't spend another night alone. He needed her, and it was past time for him to take control of this relationship he had with her.

Actually, it wasn't a relationship. It was more like on-going frustration. He couldn't sleep because he dreamed of the remembered tightness of her body clutching his. He couldn't work because the office smelled like her perfume, and he knew how much stronger it was between her pretty breasts.

He couldn't go to her because it would feed the need, yet, like a druggie, he couldn't resist one more hit. He told himself he could control it—the way he'd intended to this afternoon. Then the next thing he knew he was sitting in a meeting with a hard-on that wouldn't go away.

He turned down Amber Court and coasted to a stop in front of number twenty. He'd just talk to her. Talking wasn't touching. It didn't involve anything but voices. But he knew somehow he was going to finagle an invitation into her home.

With his decision made, Nick picked up his cell phone and had directory assistance connect him to her home phone. She answered on the second ring, breathless.

He wondered what she'd been doing. Would she welcome him tonight? It was past ten. Maybe he should hang up and just show up at her door.

"Hello? Is anyone there?" she asked.

He cleared his throat, feeling like a stalker as he sat in his car across the street from her building. "Hey, Florida girl."

"Nick."

"What's up?"

He didn't want to have to ask her if he could come over. He wanted her to say the words that might make him sound like he was in control. He'd prided himself on being the aggressive one in every relationship he'd ever had. But with Lila he was at her mercy, and, frankly, he planned to change all of that by taking back the control.

He needed to sleep with her one more time. Then he'd prove that what had happened in his office had been a fluke. The other kisses, they were part of his fascination with Lila that would end once he'd had her again.

"I've just finished up at the office."

"You sound tired," she said.

"I am." And lonely. But of course he wasn't going to admit that to her. In fact, the more he thought about it, he wasn't really lonely. He just didn't want to be alone tonight. Those were two very different things.

"I guess you're not calling for phone sex."

That surprised a laugh out of him.

"Why, have you always wanted to have phone sex?" he asked. For all her prim and proper ways, Lila had passion running deep inside of her. Even though she was afraid to let it out.

"Will it make me sound easy if I say yes?" she asked. There was a shyness to her voice that endeared her to him, though he didn't want to feel anything but lust for her. He realized suddenly that he wasn't ever going to be able to put Lila in one box and label her. She was already more to him than the women he'd dated in the past. She always would be.

He promised himself that he'd give her this. A belief in the beauty of expressing the passion she carefully hid from the world. "No. It will make you sound like just the girl I need tonight."

"Mmm. So you *were* looking for something from me."

"Yes, but not phone sex."

"Darn. Why not?"

"Because phone sex is essentially solitary and based in fantasy."

"Don't like fantasy, huh?"

"I'm ready for some more reality."

"Really?

Silence buzzed on the line. "Can I stop by?"

He sounded needy, which he hated, but there was no other option. He did need something that only she could give him. He only hoped she'd never realize how much he needed it.

"Sure. I just finished making lasagna for the next three weeks. I can heat some of it up for you. Have you eaten dinner?"

"No."

"Good. I'll feed you."

Feed my soul, he thought. He was suddenly starved. "I'll be right up."

"Where are you?"

"Across the street."

"Good thing I said yes."

"Good thing," he said, and disconnected the phone.

He crossed the street and waited for her to buzz

him in. He climbed the stairs to her apartment and her door was open.

She stood there illuminated by the light spilling from her homey apartment. Welcoming. Her long plaid skirt and long-sleeved creamy shirt created the image of vulnerability that he'd perceived the first time he saw her.

He knew he didn't deserve the sweetness that was Lila. Knew better than to believe that what she'd given him could last. Knew that he wasn't a man who'd ever be comfortable in such a homey environment because he didn't believe it was real…or that it could last.

But tonight it felt real, the way the cold did on a December morning. He saw her standing there and knew he wasn't going to be able to enter her apartment and seduce her. He wanted—no needed—for her to accept him in her bed. To want him there as much as he needed to be there.

"Lila?"

"Yeah?"

"I'm not leaving until morning."

She sighed and held out her hand. Her long fingers were warm and as she tugged him over the threshold, he heard her say, "Good."

Lila's apartment wasn't always clean, and tonight was no exception. She wished it could be like it was in the movies, where things just magically turned out right. But then real life seldom did.

It gave her pause. She wanted Nick. Had done nothing but think about him and the kiss they'd shared over his desk all afternoon, but now he was here in her cozy little place that hadn't been dusted in three weeks. Worse than that, it was laundry night and there was a pile of clean clothes on the couch.

"I'm sorry this place is such a mess."

He panned the room and she imagined the half-empty cups of tea on the counter were a bit off-putting.

"Why don't you have a seat, and I'll clean this place up?"

"Lila."

She glanced at him.

"I love your apartment. It's not messy. It's lived-in. Besides, I came to see you."

His words warmed her in a way that no one else's ever had. She didn't examine it too closely, though. Just wallowed in the feeling.

"I promised you dinner."

"Yes, you did."

She filled a plate with warm lasagna and gave him a bottle of beer. "I wish I had some bread, but I didn't bake tonight."

"This is great."

No, it wasn't. This was weird. She'd invited him in for dinner and…sex. It felt so strange. Too much pre-planning. The last time there hadn't been time to think. This time…this time, there was too much time to think.

What was she doing? She wanted to teach him to love and care. Show him that the people around him could strengthen, not weaken him. Make him believe that she was the only woman for him and instead she was hovering over him like some demented Martha Stewart wannabe trying to convince him that she was a good homemaker.

And she was failing miserably.

"Maybe you should go when you're done with dinner."

"Changed your mind?"

She shrugged. She wanted things to be perfect between them. In her head she had this image of how they should be. Her laundry didn't play into it at all.

Nick put down his fork and stood up. He came around the counter with a brisk stride, stopping only when a mere inch of space separated them. Every breath she took brushed her breasts against his chest.

"I'm not leaving unless you tell me to."

"I can't. But this feels so strange. So premeditated."

"Florida girl, you make me crazy."

He bent and kissed her. His lips brushing hers carefully, tenderly. Then the tone of his embrace changed. His hands settled on her hips, pulling her firmly against the cradle of his thighs. He rubbed his erection against her. An ache that could only be eased by Nick started at the center of her body and moved outward to every limb.

She forgot to breathe as his mouth devoured hers,

his tongue thrusting deep into her mouth. He tasted of garlic and oregano and something stronger. Something that her soul recognized as Nick.

Her entire body melted against him. He lifted her onto the counter, spreading her thighs to make room for himself. They were still separated by the barrier of her wool skirt and his pants. But she could feel the heat of him.

She rocked forward, rubbing against the hard ridge in his pants, needing from him something that was more powerful than words could describe. Something that only Nick could give, and it wasn't only physical.

His palms sliding up her thighs were rough against her skin. Her skirt bunched around her waist and he slipped his hands beneath her panties. His eyes closed and he tilted his head back, breathing harder than a racehorse that had won the derby.

Lila needed to be touching him. The emotions and sensations swamping her were too intense. She unbuttoned his shirt and caressed his chest and back. He shrugged out of it, struggling for a moment with his cufflinks, which made a pinging sound when they hit the linoleum floor.

"Take off your blouse," he ordered.

Their eyes met and held as she slowly freed the buttons on her shirt. She unbuttoned her cuffs first and then teasingly opened the front, giving him just a glimpse of the lacy camisole she wore underneath.

He bit her neck lightly and then licked the spot, sending fire shooting to her groin. She wanted to be his equal here. Wanted to tease and tempt him the way he did her. But she plain wanted him too much to wait too long.

The fire in his eyes convinced her to keep teasing. She let the fabric slip slowly down her shoulders, lifting one arm slowly out and then the other, then dropping her arms in one graceful, yet sexy, movement.

Sitting before him with only her camisole covering the top of her body and her panties covering the bottom made her feel sexy and bountiful.

"Now this," he said, stepping back so that he could watch her.

She lifted her arms above her head and slowly slid the silk and lace garment up her body. She heard his breath catch when her breasts were revealed, and by the time she'd pulled it completely off, he was back between her thighs, his mouth moving over her breast, kissing, licking and finally suckling her. She held his head close, weaved her fingers into his hair and held him to her.

He suckled both breasts in turn and the flesh between her thighs ached for his touch. Shifting forward, she rubbed herself against his hardened sex, felt him straining against the zipper.

"Lift your butt, sweetheart."

She did, and he slid her undergarment and skirt down her legs, crouching to finish removing them. Taking an ankle in each hand, he spread her legs open and stared up at her. Embarrassed, she tried to cover herself. But he stood and kissed her on the lips.

"Don't. You're so beautiful."

He whispered in her ear the things he wanted to do to her. The ways he wanted to touch her and how that made him feel like he was going to explode.

"Okay?" he asked, his voice deep and sexy.

Incapable of speech, she nodded.

He bent his head and touched her most private area with his mouth. At first just a soft touch of lips. Then he used his tongue and teeth. She rocked against his mouth, felt the tidal wave coming but didn't want to be washed away without him. Wanted to feel his heartbeat next to hers.

"Nick, come with me."

He stood and grappled in his pocket while she freed his erection. He was hot to the touch. "Not yet, Lila."

"Do you have protection this time?"

"Hell, yes."

He pulled a condom from his pocket, removed his pants and underwear, then sheathed himself and thrust into her, slowly, carefully finding his way until he was buried completely inside her body. She was so full of him. He rocked against her with building speed, his eyes watching hers, his hands gripping her hips, his chest rubbing against the aching points of her nipples.

"Come on, sweetheart," he said.

He bent his head and suckled on her neck, rocking harder and harder against her until everything in her body tightened and her body clenched around him. She couldn't breathe, couldn't think as Nick tilted her hips up and thrust so deeply she was sure he touched her womb. Then she felt him tense and watched as his climax washed through his body.

He cradled her close to him, held her as if he'd never let her go. And then, as they both came back down to earth, he lifted her high against his chest and carried her into her bedroom where he made love to her again before falling asleep in her arms. And Lila knew that he was on his way to falling in love with her. Knew that only a man who cared deeply for a woman would hold her so possessively, even in sleep. Knew that she'd found her man and her chance at happiness.

But could she convince him of that?

Seven

Lila wasn't really a morning person. That became glaringly apparent as she grumbled around her apartment trying to hurry him out the door. Nick took his time, kind of enjoying seeing this side of Lila.

He propped himself up on an elbow as she emerged from her shower. Her skin was still damp and waves of humidity filled the room. The scent of flowers surrounded him and he felt his morning erection harden even more. Damn, he wished she hadn't scurried out of bed when the alarm clock had rung.

She struggled into a red velvet robe that brought out the creamy freshness of her skin. She haphazardly piled her hair on top of her head and glared at him as she caught him smiling at her in the mirror.

He knew he should be worried about getting to work, but right now, he felt he had all the time in the world.

She left the bedroom and returned a minute later with a pile of his clothing. She tossed it on the end of the bed. "Aren't you going to get out of bed?"

He climbed to his feet and slowly put on his clothing. Aware of her gaze on him while he dressed, he glanced over his shoulder and she flushed before turning away.

"I don't have time to fix breakfast so you're on your own." She opened her closet, and he watched her careful selection. She pulled out several different outfits, held each against her body and then finally decided on one of her most severe suits.

He didn't like it. She'd chosen to wear full battle armor. The sharp black suit was one of his least favorites now that he thought about it. She always was a little harder to get along with when she wore it. He felt that it was akin to a cast-iron bra and spear. In fact, those things would seem tame next to the black suit.

It made him want to pull her back into his arms and tame her in a very masculine way. To stake a claim on her that the clothing couldn't cover and she couldn't deny. But he knew from the way she kept scowling at him that she wouldn't tolerate any sort of delays.

"I'll buy you something if you ride with me to

work,'' he said, slipping his cuff links into his pants pocket.

She frowned at him. ''I can't.''

He knew why. Despite the bonds that had been created between them, she still didn't want anyone to know that she was sleeping with him. Part of him, the callous part, didn't mind. If she were using him for sex, he'd take it. But another, deeper part minded.

''You rode to work with me last week and no one said anything.''

''That was different.'' She went into her walk-in closet to dress. She'd gone in the soft, sweet woman who'd welcomed him into her home and bed late last night and came out a superwoman. Capable of anything and not needing a mere man in her life.

''How?'' he asked.

''We hadn't...you know.'' There was the woman he'd held in his arms. The one who got flustered whenever she tried to talk about things like sex and pregnancy.

She blushed so prettily. Looked so sexy and tempting that he wanted to pull her into his arms and carry her back to bed. But he really had to leave if he was going to make it to the office on time.

''If we had the time, I'd tempt you back to bed.''

''Maybe I'd let you.'' The teasing look he received was unexpected but took the edge off what he'd been feeling.

He stalked closer to her, kissed her with the passion he'd been trying to redirect since she'd left him alone in her bed. She squirmed in his embrace, bringing her hands to the back of his head and standing on her toes.

"You'd let me," he said, coming up for air.

"I guess we'll never really know. You have to leave or you'll be late." He tried to tell himself she didn't sound smug, but he didn't believe it.

"If you hadn't spent all this time rushing me out of your bed, we'd have been able to make love again this morning."

She frowned at him until he reluctantly donned his suit jacket and headed for the door. She paced to the window and pulled the curtain back.

"Oh, my God."

"What's the matter? Did someone vandalize my car?"

"Why did you park it there?"

"Where else would I park?"

"I don't know. Not there. Everyone who drives by will see it."

"It's not like there's a big flashing neon sign over it, Lila."

"But some of the girls who live here work at Colette. They might recognize your car."

"So?"

"I like to think of them as my friends."

"My Porsche out front won't change that."

"Yes," she said, quietly. "It will."

"You have to stop worrying about what others

think. If these women give you a hassle about me spending the night then they aren't your friends."

"They won't have to say anything. But I'll know."

"Lila, believe in yourself and your choices. You're the only one you can please. Believe me, I learned that a long time ago."

"From your parents?"

"In an indirect way."

"Don't you ever wish you had someone else to lean on?"

"No. Then I'd have a liability."

"Caring about people isn't a liability."

"It can be," he said, and walked out the door. Lila would never understand how those softer emotions could chain a man until he couldn't stand on his own.

Lila was still shaken two hours later by what Nick had revealed on his way out the door. The office was still abuzz with rumors and speculation. Lila wished she'd called in sick so she wouldn't have to face Nick today. But he was busy in meetings anyway.

Caring is a liability. The words circled in her head like vultures, and she tried to calm herself, but she knew that they were pecking the heck out of her relationship with Nick. They didn't really have a relationship when you got down to it. What they had was hot sex once in awhile.

She leaned back in her chair and wrapped her arms around her body. She knew she was taking a gamble, hoping she could teach him to love, but she'd never realized how great the risk was. Until now.

Picking up the phone she dialed her mom's number. She needed to let the joy and love her mother felt for her wash over her. But her mom was at work and Lila got the machine. She didn't leave a message and hung up not feeling as if she'd resolved anything.

The brooch Rose had given her was pinned to her lapel. The gems shone brighter against the stark black backdrop. She'd worn the suit because it made her feel professional and in control. It also made her feel invincible.

Which hadn't helped at all when Meredith had mentioned hearing a man's voice in the hall last night. Was it someone visiting her or Mr. Parkes who lived in 3B? Lila pretended it was Mr. Parkes, but she'd hated lying.

Then again, she'd hate to lose the friendship she'd started with the women in her apartment building because she was having an affair with her boss. Damn, it sounded like a cliché but it felt real. Too real sometimes.

She wasn't ashamed of anything she'd done with Nick the night before, wasn't really ashamed to have others know they were seeing each other. But she was uncomfortable with the fact that he'd pretty much told her he'd never marry her.

The phone rang. "Nick Camden's office, this is Lila."

"This is the seniors' center. Is Mr. Camden there?"

"He's in a meeting. Can I take a message?"

"Yes, please have him call right away."

"What's this regarding?"

"Mr. McKee."

"What happened?"

"A minor stroke, but we couldn't get in touch with his son, and Mr. Camden is our second contact. Mr. McKee's at the hospital now. Having family around at his age can really make a difference."

"Yes…I'll let him know. Right away." She hung up the phone.

Lila's legs were shaking. She didn't want to pass the message on to Nick but knew she had to. He was in the building, probably on the executive level in the boardroom. She'd page him.

She typed a bland message into his alpha pager for him to call her right away and three minutes later he walked in the door. He looked hurried and stressed but not tired. In fact, a gleam entered his eye when he saw her. She thrilled at seeing it there.

Focusing herself on preparing to tell him bad news was hard. She never knew the right thing to do. "Sorry to pull you out of the meeting."

"I was hoping you would. What's up?"

"Oh, gosh. Nick sit down."

The gleam left his eyes and his shoulders straightened. He skimmed her body, staring for a minute at her stomach. "Just tell me your news."

Her news? She wouldn't page him out of a meeting

to tell him she'd started her period. "It's not *my* news, Nick."

"Lila, I'm tired because we didn't sleep much last night. I want you on my desk again and I have to get back to that meeting before tempers explode and irreparable damage is done. Just tell me why you paged me."

"The seniors' center called. Mr. McKee had a stroke. He's at the hospital."

His face didn't go ashen. In fact, no emotion was revealed there at all. Instead he shut down. Lila was ready to offer the comfort of her arms, but the man standing before her was a stranger. And not someone who'd welcome solace from her.

"I'm going over there. Call Judy, Xavier's secretary, and tell her I won't be coming back today. Then ask Phillips to call me in the car. I'll brief him on what's going on and he can attend the afternoon session of meetings with the board."

She picked up the phone and made the calls. She finished just as Nick came out of his office, briefcase in hand.

"I've got my pager and cell phone. If you need me, don't hesitate to call."

"Nick, is there anything I can do?" she asked, wishing she could go with him, even if only to sit next to him in the waiting room. But she had a job to do here.

"No," he said, with a finality that made her ache. She touched his arm as he walked by her. Nick glanced down at her hand on his jacket sleeve. "He'll be okay."

"No, Lila, he won't. He'll never be the same again even if he recovers."

"They said *minor* stroke," she said.

"But the message was the same," he said, taking her hand in his and pulling her closer.

"What message?" she asked. His eyes revealed the pain that he hid through confidence and disdain.

"Life is unexpected," he muttered.

Yes, it is, she thought. Because she'd never have expected Nick to be the kind of person who'd care so deeply about an elderly man. She'd never have expected Nick to want more than one night with her. She'd never have expected that Colette's problems would seem small compared to what was happening in her own life.

"That's not a bad thing."

"It's not a good thing, either."

"I know you don't believe that, Nick," she said, not willing to let him leave unchallenged.

"Yes, I do."

"What we have is unexpected," she said, and immediately wished she could call back the words.

He stared at her for a moment then moved to the door. "It's not lasting, either."

His words echoed in her mind as he walked away. She sank to her chair, telling herself that he was hurting right now. That the only adult who'd cared about him in his childhood was sick, and it was anger that made him react. But in her heart she feared that those words reflected feelings she couldn't change.

The luminous dial on his watch read eleven o'clock. Visiting hours had ended a few hours ago, and Nick had been relegated to the hallway waiting area. The waiting area was light, with big fluorescent lamps that seemed too bright for the ICU.

Nick rubbed his eyes and leaned back against the wall. Buster was flying in from Hawaii, but it would be about six hours until he arrived. Nick had assured his friend he'd stay. There were some debts that he'd go to any length to repay.

His life was such a jumble of confusion right now that nothing seemed normal. When he thought he saw Lila walking toward him it seemed surreal. He knew he must be hallucinating because after he'd told her what they had wouldn't last he'd expected her never really to talk to him again.

And who could blame her? He'd acted like an ass, the way he often did when he felt vulnerable. It always yielded the same results, injuring someone he'd never want to hurt. And causing Lila pain was a double-edged sword because it made him ache, as well.

She paused in front of him, and he knew she was no illusion. His body was on red alert, senses so attuned to her scent that they sent arousal rushing through him. She wore a plaid miniskirt and black tights that made her legs seem endless. But he knew they weren't. He was intimately acquainted with where they ended and met.

"Lila," he said. Just her name, hoping for some vocal confirmation that he wasn't having one hell of a daydream. After the day he'd had it would probably turn into a vicious nightmare that would scare the socks off even Stephen King.

"I brought you dinner," she said. Lila was so…homey. She reminded him of what he'd wanted his mom to be when he was growing up. The basket in her hands was wrapped in a towel and a tantalizing aroma filled the air. But at the same time she was a sexy siren who could make him forget about family and focus only on her.

"You shouldn't have."

He meant it. He didn't deserve her sweet caring. And he knew that she cared about him. Because if he'd learned one thing about Lila the woman, it was that she wasn't the type to sleep with a man she couldn't care about. More than just physical passion had brought her to him.

"I knew you wouldn't eat. Have you even left this hallway since he was brought in?"

"Yes," he said. He'd had to use the restroom earlier this afternoon.

"Why don't you sit down? I brought some cottage pie."

He started to say no, but there was a light in her eyes that warned against it. She was offering him an olive branch. He should take it and be happy that he'd gotten off so easily.

Except that he couldn't. He shouldn't be let off the hook that easily. And tonight had reminded him of some irrevocable facts, some truths in life he'd been conveniently ignoring while he'd enjoyed Lila. Today he'd realized he could bury his head no more.

"Why are you here?"

She shrugged and set her basket on one of the cloth-covered chairs. "I don't know. I tried to stay at home, but all I did was think about you."

"I'm not the right guy for you, Lila. Today made that brutally clear to me."

She propped her hands on her hips and tilted her head to glance up at him. "You can be so stubborn sometimes."

"I know."

"Don't you even care that this could be your once in a lifetime?"

"It's not. I already had that, remember?"

"Yeah. Sit down and eat before this gets cold."

"I'm not hungry."

"I don't believe you."

Suddenly, the knowledge that she wanted him and he couldn't keep her overwhelmed him. He reached out and pulled her close to him. He felt her rise on her toes. He bent his head close and rested his forehead against hers.

"I *am* hungry, Lila. There is a hunger so deep in my soul that I doubt even you could ever fill it. You keep pushing until I think maybe you could, but I know better. Today proved it. It was a careless comment, but I meant it. I'm not your forever man.''

"But you could be, Nick, and that's why I'm here.''

He didn't want to take the chance he'd hurt her again, maybe even worse this time. "I don't know any other way.''

"I'm trying to show you.''

He sighed. She had a relentless streak that he'd never noticed before. It annoyed him. "Lila, what do you want from me?''

She brushed her lips against his. "A chance.''

Don't ask, he told himself. There were some things a man wasn't meant to know about. The inside of a woman's purse, the things she did in the bathroom and the secrets of her soul.

But he needed to know what secrets she was keeping. Needed to hear the words that would be like manna to his starving soul. Needed to know if what she felt was as real as she'd hinted.

"A chance at what?''

"Forever.''

Damn, that's what he'd been afraid of. He wasn't a forever kind of guy. Had tried it with disastrous results. He wasn't even sure he was a forever boss with the turmoil at Colette. He started to speak, planned to turn her down. But she put her forefinger against his lips and stopped the words before they could form.

"I'm willing to start with now."

"Now, I can handle," he said. In fact, now was what he needed from her. He tugged her closer to his embrace and held her for a long time, not letting go until Buster arrived. As Lila walked away, Nick felt for the first time that the future held something other than work and a cold, lonely existence.

Eight

According to Lila's somewhat unscientific calculations her period was a day late. Normally she would have been thankful, because she hated it. She loved it when she skipped a month or two, as was sometimes the case. But this month, with her new relationship with Nick as fragile as a porcelain Ming vase, she wanted it to start.

She couldn't stay with Nick if she were pregnant and he didn't want to marry her. Nick hadn't been kidding about never remarrying. There was something very serious in his eyes when he talked about the past, something he hadn't done since that night in the hospital.

But here she was on a Saturday morning in the

Home Depot, helping Nick pick out paint for his guest bedroom. She'd offered to help him with his redecorating when he mentioned how much he liked her place. The compliment had thrilled her and she'd eagerly volunteered to help him.

"They should be done mixing the paint in a few minutes. Want to come with me to get the supplies?"

"Sure." She followed him down another aisle admiring the way his faded jeans hugged his butt when he bent over to grab a pack of paintbrushes. Her fingers tingled with the need to pat him right there. To just reach out and feel his firmness, maybe give him a little pinch.

"Lila?"

"Yes?"

"Florida girl, what are you thinking?"

"Nothing."

"That's not what the blush on your face is telling me."

"You've got great buns, Camden. What can I say?"

Now he flushed, and she was pleased. "You were eyeing me?"

"Yes. And I was thinking of copping a feel."

Pivoting, he bent down again to pick up a paint tray. "Don't let me stop you."

This was the Nick she wanted to see more of. The man who forgot the pain of the past and let down his guard. Without even looking to see if there was anyone else on the aisle with them, she reached out and caressed his backside. Firm, taut and utterly masculine. She traced the pocket of his jeans and then lightly scraped her fingernail over the center seam.

"That's enough," he said, grabbing her hand and facing her. His erection distended the front of his jeans. She slid her fingers over the button fly.

For a minute he held her hand closer to his arousal, then he pulled her down the aisle after him. She felt a bit naughty and loved the feeling of power that came with it.

"What's the matter?" she asked teasingly.

"Nothing that you can't fix as soon as we get out of here."

"I'm not sure I can solve your problem. It looks hard to me."

"I am." She melted when he glanced over his shoulder, his eyes a promise of carnal delights. She loved the feel of him moving over her in bed. He always made love to her as if she were the most precious thing in the world to him. He also made her feel like the sexiest woman he'd ever held.

They rounded the corner and Rose was standing there at the paint counter. Lila forgot all about teasing Nick. Forgot all about how good he made her feel inside. All she could focus on now was explaining herself to Rose.

She tugged Nick to a stop but it was too late. Rose glanced up from the paint chips she was studying and caught Lila's eye. Lila pulled her hand free from Nick's and tried to appear circumspect but knew she'd failed miserably. Desire pumped through her veins and her pulse seemed to be dictating that all of her thoughts center on Nick.

"Lila, what a pleasant surprise."

"Hi, Rose."

"And who's this?" Rose asked.

"Umm, this is Nick Camden. My boss."

Nick gave her a sideways glance, but didn't say anything, just walked over to the counter to get the paint. She watched him leave knowing she'd disappointed him.

"Wasn't he with you at the drugstore last week?"

"Yes, he was, Rose."

"Has my brooch brought you luck then?"

"I don't know, Rose."

"That man doesn't look at you like he's only your boss."

Lila had hoped she could hide her personal life from the people who were important to her. Her mom, Rose, the women of Amber Court, Charlotte and Myrtle at the senior center. But she realized she wasn't fooling anyone.

"Please don't think that this is improper in any way."

"Honey, I was young once, too."

Lila looked at Rose. "I think you still are."

"Thanks, sweetie."

"I've been meaning to give you back your brooch. Will you be home this afternoon?"

"Yes, but you keep it for a while longer. Will I see you for dinner tomorrow night?"

Lila nodded. Rose had her, Jayne, Sylvie and Meredith over for dinner once a month. When she'd first moved to Indiana it had been a lifesaver, and in some ways it still was. Those ladies had become very important to her, just as Rose had. She thought about her relationship with Nick and realized she didn't want to lose him either. But she would if she kept pushing him away.

"Ready, Lila?" Nick asked. Lila nodded and waved goodbye to Rose. Nick didn't say anything to her until they'd gotten into his car. He stowed the paint cans behind her seat and then sat there without starting the motor.

"When are you going to trust me enough to stop pretending to others that I'm nothing but your boss?"

She knew it was a matter of trust, and it seemed wrong for him to question her trust when he was so lacking in it himself. "You're the one who said it wasn't forever."

"You're the one who said it could be. But apparently one of us was lying and one was telling the truth."

She slunk back against the seat. She didn't know what to say. She'd been urging him out of his shell, daring him to put his fears on the line while she'd stayed comfortably hidden behind her own. No guts, no glory, she thought. She couldn't ask him for everything and give only half in return.

"You're right. From now on I'm not hiding."

"You're sure?"

"Yes," she said. And to prove it she kissed him there in the car, in front of anyone who happened to be walking by in the parking lot. The act was freeing and Lila knew she'd never be the same.

The next evening, Lila hurried down to Rose's apartment. Of all the things she liked about her life in Indiana, the friendships she'd formed with Meredith, Jayne and Sylvie were perhaps the most important. To Lila it was as if she'd found the sisters she'd never had. Though she sometimes felt like she didn't fit in the group, she wouldn't miss their monthly dinners for anything.

She hesitated at the door. Her relationship with Nick played heavily on her mind. Would this be something she'd have to sacrifice if it became common knowledge that she was dating him?

She didn't want to think about that. She hoped that things wouldn't change, but the past had proven that life always did.

She knocked on the door and Meredith opened it. Meredith had the kind of natural beauty that most women would kill for, but she kept it carefully hidden. She could be a real knockout if only she'd dress a little better and maybe get some contact lenses. But Meredith's looks mattered little to Lila because underneath those baggy clothes was one of the nicest women Lila had ever met.

"Everyone else is here. I was just about ready to run up and get you." Meredith took the pie from Lila's hands and placed it on the kitchen counter.

"Sorry I'm late," Lila said.

"No problem," Rose replied, coming out of the kitchen.

Soon they were all seated around the table. Jayne kept the conversation going. She was her usual bubbly self and had even more energy than ever now that she'd found a solid man. Lila was envious of her friend, wondering if Nick and she would ever find a happy place in their relationship.

Sylvie brought the conversation around to work and no one really said much about the situation. Lila was glad because some of the things she knew were still confidential.

"Is the charity auction still taking place?" Rose asked.

"Yes. Nick said that the company wants the community to know that nothing at Colette has changed. The new jewelry designs are to die for. I almost wish I was going to be modeling this year. But I'm too involved in the planning."

"Yes, but you'd have to go out with one of those men," Meredith said.

"That wouldn't be too bad," Jayne said.

"Only because you have a man. The rest of us are fair game," Sylvie said.

"I don't think of myself so much as game as a lame duck," Lila said. She always felt a bit out of

her element with these women. At her own level she
was confident, but these three were very successful
and she didn't even want to compare herself to Rose.

"Would you do it, Rose?"

"In a heartbeat."

"Well, it'll be lovely. I know that much since I'm
in charge of the decor. So are either of you thinking
of volunteering for the auction block?" Lila asked,
looking at Meredith and Sylvie.

Sylvie shook her head and Meredith stood to col-
lect the dinner dishes. "Who's ready for dessert?"
she asked.

They shared the pie and coffee and then retired to
the living room to chat for a little while longer. Lila
left earlier than she normally would have, but she
wanted to get home in case Nick had called her. He
was out of town and she missed the sound of his
voice. That was something she didn't want to think
about too much.

Nick returned from a three-day sales trip to Boston.
The office was still standing, but Lila wasn't at her
desk. It was 4:30. She might already be gone.

Damn. He'd flown standby on an earlier flight just
to get back in time to see her. He hadn't planned on
stopping by her apartment on the way home. Though
he did plan to spend the night with her.

He didn't want to upset her again by leaving his
car parked on the street. But that was something

they'd have to deal with. She'd said she wasn't hiding anymore and he was going to hold her to that.

Her phone was forwarded to Xavier's assistant and Nick found out from her that Lila was at a planning meeting for the annual charity auction. A surge of possessiveness flooded him, knowing that the women who worked for Colette were often the ones who volunteered for the auction block. Lila wasn't going to be one of them, he vowed. She belonged to him.

She hadn't convinced him that *forever* was meant for them, but he knew that *now* was. And next month would be too soon for him to let go of her. A weary part of his soul urged him to create more distance between them. But the hunger for her was too great. After so many years of emotional starvation he'd finally found a woman who could feed him, and he was needy enough to hang on to her whether it was wise or not.

Over the three days he was gone she should have gotten her period. He was torn. More than anything in the world he'd love to have a son to teach to waterski and play baseball. Or a small daughter who'd be a reflection of Lila's sense of style and his own love of the outdoors. But with a keen sense of self-preservation, he hoped she wasn't pregnant.

Their relationship was like a leaky houseboat. On the surface it looked great, and each was careful to not rock the boat, but water was slowly seeping inside, and both of them were aware that sooner or later they were going to have to bail.

Yet every time they were together, he, who'd always prided himself on enjoying the peace that a life of routine could bring, enjoyed the tempest. Lila was by turns sexy and unpredictable, heart-touching and heart-wrenching. She was every woman and at the same time the only woman in the world for him.

And that scared him. He didn't like the emotions she brought to the surface. Didn't like the way she'd managed to make him care for her when caring was the last thing he needed. Didn't like that she was the first person he thought of when he woke up in the morning and the last face he saw before he drifted off to sleep.

He didn't think their working relationship would survive that obsession. He knew that Lila thought they could last forever but Nick was more cynical. He'd never known anything that had touched him to withstand life. He wasn't sure if this could even survive the turmoil at Colette. Sooner or later something was going to happen to drive a wedge through the crack already there. And the past had taught him that nothing would be able to repair it.

Nick entered his office and stopped to stare at his desk. In the center was a picnic-style basket and a thick brown blanket.

"Well, what have we here?" Nick muttered to himself. He dropped his briefcase on the floor and loosened his tie as he opened the basket.

Inside were food containers, a bottle of California merlot, two wineglasses and eating utensils. And, as he shifted around the contents, he realized there was a condom packet on the very bottom.

Seemed as if Lila had a surprise for him. He hoped he hadn't ruined it. He pivoted to exit his office. He'd wait for Lila by her desk.

"Who's in here?" Lila asked from the door.

"I am."

She flushed as she glanced from him to the open picnic basket. She was wearing a brown suit that should have looked dull but on her was vibrant. She was an all-American dream of home and family. Her blond hair was tied at the back of her neck. She was the end of summer and the promise of snuggling by a warm fire through winter.

"Welcome back," she said with a tender smile. It was the kind of smile he'd seen on her face only after they'd made love. His pulse beat faster, and his blood heated.

"Thanks. Did you get me a gift?" he asked, gesturing to the basket contents.

"Maybe. Maybe not," she said, walking into the room and closing the door behind her. Her hips swayed lazily with each step she took. Her skirt had a slit he hadn't noticed until she moved. It went halfway up her thigh. His fingers tingled with the need to touch her. And his groin strained against his inseam until he could feel his pulse in it.

"If not me, then who?"

She stopped next to him. Nibbling on her bottom

lip she pulled containers from the basket. "Maybe it's for Mr. McKee. Hospital food's not great."

Nick reached in front of her, deliberately brushing his arms against her breasts. Her intake of breath was his reward.

"I'm not sure he can eat all of this."

"You might be right."

Then Nick found what he'd been searching for and pulled the prophylactic from the bottom. "I'm sure they wouldn't let him use this."

"Well…"

He bent down to nuzzle her neck. "It had better be for me."

"And if it isn't?"

"I'll have to convince you I'm the only man you want to share it with."

"It might take a lot of effort on your part."

"I'm up for it."

She reached down and cupped his erection. "You certainly are."

She slipped her arms around his neck, and Nick took her mouth with the pent-up frustration of a man who knew that he was holding sunlight and winter was looming around the corner.

He made love to her on the surface of his desk and this time was so much better than the last. As he climaxed he clung to her with a desperation he would have denied, but in his heart he knew she was slipping away and he was helpless to keep her where he wanted her. *In his arms.*

* * *

The next afternoon, Lila grabbed a pre-made salad from the lunch counter and paid for it. The cafeteria was crowded but not noisy. The strain of the possible takeover had grown in the offices of Colette, Inc., but Lila realized it had also been spreading. A group of six men and women were talking about the takeover as Lila walked by.

"I heard that the executives are all cutting deals to save their own hides."

Lila paused to hear what the man had to say. She knew it was rude to eavesdrop, but she hadn't heard any rumors about the executives yet.

"Xavier's not going to be able to save himself. Grey probably won't keep any of the board."

"Nick Camden's been courting Grey," one of the women said.

"He has not," Lila interrupted.

"Who are you?"

"Nick's secretary. And I can tell you he's not interested in working for anyone who'd tear Colette apart."

"Yeah, right. What promises has he made you?" said one of the men.

"The same ones he's made to his entire staff. That he'll do everything in his power to make sure Marcus Grey is unsuccessful in his bid to take over Colette."

"And you believe him?"

"Yes, I do."

"I wonder why you're so loyal to him."

Lila told herself to leave. To just walk away before she said something she'd regret. But she knew she'd never regret defending Nick. He was a good, kind man and he didn't deserve to be talked about as if he were the villain in this scenario.

"Because he's an honest man, a good man. He won't go down without a fight."

"We're not doubting that. Just who is he going to be fighting for, himself or the company?"

"Colette is important to Nick." How could she convince them that Colette was the only thing that Nick really believed in? He'd dedicated his life to this company.

"Whatever you say. We'll just have to wait and see."

Lila spun on her heel and marched out of the cafeteria. Tears burned the backs of her eyes. She wasn't sure why she'd made such a big deal about Nick. She should have just kept walking.

But she hadn't been able to. She'd never spoken out for herself when she'd been picked on in school or unfairly judged because of the way she looked. But when it came to someone she cared about, she wouldn't let them be maligned.

When she got back to her desk she sat in her chair, anger vibrating through her. There was no way she was going to be able to work today. No way she was going to be able to see Nick and not tell him what had happened. Because she was still outraged that he'd been the topic of malicious gossip.

But more than outrage flowed through her. Though she didn't want to admit it she knew in the back of her mind those comments had raised some doubt. Why wasn't Nick more concerned about the takeover attempt?

"Lila, are you back from lunch?" Nick yelled from his office.

No matter how high up the rungs you climbed, the boss always liked to be able to yell for his secretary. She'd given up pointing out that he had an intercom on his phone, it was easier to call for her, he'd said.

"I'm here," she said, dropping her salad in one of her desk drawers. Maybe she'd eat it later.

"If you have a minute, I need you to take a memo."

"Sure." She went into his office and took the dictation. It was a policy change for international travel and when Nick was finished she hovered in the doorway unable to leave.

"What's up?" he asked.

She knew she should leave but she wasn't going to be happy until she knew. "Do you know Marcus Grey?"

He raised one eyebrow at the question. "I know who he is, but I've never met him. Why do you ask?"

His answer made her glad she'd spoken up earlier. She knew Nick wouldn't try to cut a deal. "I was just trying to figure out why he was doing this."

"Don't make it personal, Lila. He's a businessman

and Colette is a profit-generating company. I'm sure his interest is purely monetary.''

''Then why didn't he approach the board outright?''

''We're a tightly held company. You know that. He may have thought that was the only way.''

''Is that what you'd do?'' she asked.

He leaned back in his chair. ''Hell, no. I lack subtlety.''

''Yeah, you do.'' The last of her doubts melted away. Nick was more in-your-face than that. He wouldn't conspire behind her back or behind Xavier's.

''Thanks a lot.''

''I'm glad you aren't subtle.''

''Why?''

''A sneaky man wouldn't have seduced me on his desk and forgotten about protection.''

His eyes narrowed, but he didn't seem angry. ''How are we doing on that front?''

''No period yet,'' she said, flushing a little.

''Did you use that test kit?''

''Yes, but it didn't turn either pink or blue. I'm going to pick another one up on my way home from work.''

''I'll take you.''

''You don't have to.''

''I don't like you taking the bus after work,'' he said.

The possessiveness in his tone warmed her. "I drove my car today."

"I thought you hated to drive?"

"I hate the cold more. It was freezing this morning."

"If you'd stayed with me last night you wouldn't have had to drive."

"I know."

"Stay with me tonight," he said.

She hesitated. She had the feeling that her defense of him in the cafeteria was going to ruin any chance she had of pretending they were nothing more than co-workers, but that aside, she'd already decided to be open about her relationship with Nick.

"Please," he said.

And she couldn't say no.

Nine

Nick heard of Lila's defense of him as he was leaving the building later that day. Just a casual comment on the elevator from the Director of Domestic Marketing, but it changed Nick's world. No longer could he doubt even the slightest that Lila was committed to him. And she deserved the same commitment from him. She deserved to know that he wanted her in his life.

Her late period made him believe they were going to be parents. And he realized that was exactly what he wanted. He couldn't offer her marriage. Wasn't about to tempt those fates again by tying his name to a woman's, but he thought that he and Lila could have a good life without marriage.

Marriage was a piece of paper and what they had didn't require approval from the outside. Lila might be ready to accept that. He glanced at his watch. Lila wasn't due at his house until eight. That gave him two hours to make everything as perfect as he could.

Lila had been important to him for a long time. She helped him run his division by keeping him on track and balancing his wild impulses with a sense of sanity.

He knew she could bring the same thing to his personal life. And it was something that had been missing for a long, long time. Something he didn't think he'd ever had. It was as if he was alive for the first time.

He called his favorite restaurant and ordered a gourmet dinner. He stopped by the florist and picked up an exotic-looking bouquet that was as unique as the woman he planned to give it to. Then he drove to his house. The exclusive neighborhood catered to the up and coming. It was a posh area that made Nick feel as if he'd crossed a barrier and achieved something his parents wouldn't have believed he could attain. Maybe they would have changed their minds if they'd lived to see him graduate from college. But a drunk driver had assured they wouldn't.

The house was too big for a bachelor but would suit a family. He could easily see Lila having more than one child. His six-bedroom home would hold whatever her dream family was. He made a mental note to ask about her dreams of the future. The ones he'd never asked about before because the woman who didn't want anyone to see her with him wasn't someone he could build a tomorrow with.

His place was neat, thanks to the maid service he employed, and, after some scrounging, he found a pair of silver candlesticks and some long tapered candles. He'd never needed to seduce anyone before and had no idea how to go about it. But he knew Lila. Knew what it took to seduce her senses. She was a fantasy girl. She wanted the fairy tale, and tonight he'd give it to her.

He laid a fire in the fireplace and changed from his suit into chinos and a casual shirt. Lila arrived just as the delivery boy was walking back toward his car. She looked sweet and sexy and his heart lurched when she walked into his house.

She wore a silk blouse and slim-fitting skirt that ended mid-calf. She was a picture of respectability. Her powerful, feminine scent surrounded him, making him feel very masculine and primitive. The delivery boy smiled at her and Nick wanted to brand Lila as his. Wanted to mark her in some way that all other men who glanced at her would immediately know she belonged to him.

And that wasn't a comfortable thought. He didn't like the possessiveness. Didn't trust the emotions roiling through him like a thunderstorm gathering strength and wreaking havoc on the unsuspecting flowers and trees.

He pulled her to him, putting his arms around her.

She glanced up at him with a warm smile that made him hard. Her touches and gazes went through his control with an ease that would have been embarrassing if he didn't know that he affected her the same way.

She glowed in the moonlight and Nick was suddenly aware that they were alone inside his big empty house.

The heavy-metal emotion of Creed played in the background. Not exactly seduction music, but hey, Lila was early. She hummed along with one of the songs as she helped him set the food on the table. The feeling of losing control gained strength, and Nick motioned for her to sit down.

He lit the tapers and switched to a Harry Connick, Jr. CD, one he knew to be Lila's favorite.

The crooner sang of love and Nick knew better than to believe him, but tonight he liked the fairy tale. He filled both of their glasses with some French champagne he'd been given on a recent business trip. "To the most beautiful woman in the world."

She met his gaze, something that Europeans always did during a toast but he'd noticed most Americans didn't. It was a mark of the kind of woman Lila was. Whenever they were together, she created an oasis for him. A place where he could let slip the tight rein of his control and be himself, whether he wanted to or not.

Most of the time that bothered him, but tonight he felt safe. Safe from the prying eyes of his peers. Safe from the battle his parents had waged trying to use him to wound each other. Safe from the base emotions she called to the surface.

She tipped her head to the side. "I'm not good at toasts."

"Then just say, *Salud!*"

"If you give me a minute..."

"Tonight we have nothing but time."

She smiled. Her eyes glowed in the candlelight, and he saw in them something he'd never seen in a woman's eyes before. He couldn't define it, he only knew that it made him feel stronger and better than he was.

"To a man who embodies everything a man should be."

Nick knew there was no way he could live up to that. He didn't even know what she expected a man to be. Knowing that her father had left before she was born and that she'd been mistreated by the boys in her hometown, he feared he wouldn't be able to live up to her expectations.

"What are these qualities?" he asked.

"Just what you are, Nick. A noble man of integrity and truth."

Damn. Hard words to live up to. But he knew that for Lila, he'd try. No matter what, he'd always try to be truthful and act with integrity.

The champagne and rich French cuisine left Lila feeling voluptuous. Her senses were heightened and she felt as if her entire being was pulsing. The evening felt like a moment out of a dream and she reveled in it and in Nick.

"Ready for dessert?" Nick asked.

Lila nodded, afraid to trust her voice. Nick left the room for a minute and returned with a tray of coffee and French silk pie. Lila offered to pour the coffee but Nick brushed her hands aside.

She felt pampered as she ate the chocolate dessert and drank her coffee laced with Frangelico. She'd never felt like this before. The candles cast them both in a soft glow and it was as though they were in one of those dream sequences that you see sometimes in a movie or sitcom. Of course, in a sitcom it turns out to be a vicious joke. She'd never been able to laugh when the romantic scene turned to a nightmare, because it cut too close to her version of reality. It cut too close to the way she knew most men could behave. But not tonight. Tonight it felt like the real thing, and if she were deluding herself, she'd live with that illusion until tomorrow morning.

The Harry Connick, Jr., CD had switched over to Sade singing her lush songs of love and its sometimes bittersweet reward, but tonight Lila heard no warning. She felt the music in her heart, and, as she stared across the table at Nick, she felt as if he'd become part of her body as well. She felt as if their souls had intertwined to become one complete person, if only for this one night.

It was as if reality had ceased to exist and they

lived in a world of just the two of them. A sensual world, she realized, as Nick leaned forward and brushed his finger over her bottom lip.

"You had a crumb."

All evening he'd touched her in little ways that, taken separately, wouldn't have amounted to much. But together they were slowly bringing a heat to her body she'd never experienced before.

"Did you get them all?" she asked.

He leaned forward and stroked his tongue across her lips. His warmth, the taste of coffee and the pulsing of desire pounded through her.

"There we go," he said, and sat back.

She wanted to crawl across the table and pull his head to hers. To ravage his mouth in a way she'd never ravaged any man's before. Wanted to make him finish what these teasing touches had been leading up to.

He'd created something here tonight that she'd never sensed in him. She wouldn't have guessed Nick could find and light candles. Wouldn't have imagined he'd take the time to order a nice dinner.

Wouldn't have known that he'd be so good at seduction. Except that it felt more personal. Not like something he'd done for other women, but something he did only for her.

"Why all of this?" she asked, feeling like a fairy-tale princess who'd spent her life taking care of herself.

He finished his champagne in one swallow. "I wanted to repay you."

That stung—the evening of her secret dreams was a payback. She clenched her fingers into fists in her lap. Her nails bit into her palms, and she knew she shouldn't ask. Should just smile and thank him for the dinner. Should just pretend it didn't hurt but she couldn't. "For what?"

"For defending me. I've always been alone and today...I don't know how to express what I felt."

Disappointment laced with anger raced through her. When was she going to learn that men didn't go out of their way to seduce her? "You mean at work?"

"Yes."

She frowned at him. "But that was a job thing."

"No, it wasn't. It was because of what we have. It's because you had the chance to know me away from the office that you defended me. Thank you."

His words made her believe that what they had was special and made her realize that she wouldn't have defended Nick the boss if she hadn't known Nick the man. Had she done something today that had far-reaching repercussions? Something she hadn't even realized she'd been doing?

"It was nothing. They were just spouting off."

"But you did something I know is hard for you."

She shivered to think he knew her so well. That he'd taken the time to look beyond the surface. She knew then that this evening wasn't a conscience gift but a gift from Nick to her. "What was that?"

"You drew attention to yourself and to us."

She wasn't ready to deal with those consequences yet. She'd spent the afternoon sequestered in the office avoiding others, but she knew that couldn't last. "I couldn't walk away without saying something."

"I know." The quiet certainty in his voice touched her. She slid out of her chair and walked around next to him. Needing to touch him, she cupped his jaw and ran the ball of her thumb over his lips. His sharp intake of breath made her breasts feel heavier and her blood heat even more.

"What else do you know?" she asked.

He bit her thumb and held her flesh captive for a moment, nibbling on it. "That if I don't make love to you tonight I will go insane."

"Well, we don't want that."

"No, we don't. I've been imagining you on my bed since the first time we made love."

"Then let's fulfill your fantasy," she said.

"I hope we'll get to some of your fantasies as well."

Nick stood and lifted her in his arms. Lila knew that they'd already met and filled her fantasies. The man who'd orchestrated this evening wasn't a man intent on having a fling. This was a man who could make a lifetime commitment, baby or no baby. And that made Lila's heart pulse to life for the first time ever.

Nick had wanted Lila in his bed for so long that when he lowered her onto the navy counterpane, he had to step back and really look at her there. The light spilling from the hallway painted her in shadows. And for a moment Nick wondered if she were really there at all. Maybe she was only an illusion that would disappear the first time he tried to touch her.

Her long blond hair contrasted with the darkness of the bedspread and pillows. She flung her arms out to either side and lay there before him. Legs slightly parted, her skirt high on her thighs. She kicked her shoes off and opened her arms, welcoming him.

Lust inflamed him, his sex had never felt as engorged as it did while he watched her on the bed. Though he knew the secrets her body held, she seemed to embody everything mysterious about women. And in that moment she was the only woman to his man.

He stepped out of his loafers, hand going to his belt buckle. He wanted tonight to be special, a slow seduction of the senses, but with Lila there was no gentling. It was an intense rush that encompassed not only his body but also his soul.

"Tonight is for you," he said, hoping saying the words would give him the control he needed to make this one of the slow and tender times.

"I hope it's for you, too."

"It is."

"Then come here. I'm lonely without you."

He let his belt fall to the floor and pulled his shirt from the waistband of his pants, but otherwise left all of his clothing on. Lila reached for the buttons on the front of her blouse but he stilled her hands.

"I've always enjoyed unwrapping my presents."

"A present, am I?"

The sweetest one he'd ever received, but he didn't say the words out loud. Instead he just unfastened her shirt and then slipped it off her body. She was heart-stoppingly lovely in the pale light of the moon. Her silk and lace bra cupped the alabaster globes of her breasts as a lover would. As he planned to. Her nipples beaded against the fabric and Nick couldn't wait another moment to taste her.

Bending down, he nipped lightly at her nipple before suckling her. She moaned and her fingers tunneled through his hair, holding him to her. He relished her touch. Her hands slipped from his head down his neck and then to the front of his shirt.

He leaned back and ripped it over his head. She watched him through half-closed eyes as he returned to her. He reached down and unfastened her bra. He slid it down her arms and she lifted a little to help but he left it at her wrists, effectively chaining her arms behind her.

"Nick?"

"Trust me?"

"Yes," she said, the word a sigh.

He rubbed his chest against her bare breasts with their hardened nipples, feeling the impact to his soul. He supported her with a hand under her shoulders so that her wrists weren't strained. Her hips rose from the bed, nestling against his hardness.

He bent and took her mouth, kissing her as if he'd never tasted her before. He nibbled around the edges of her mouth until she groaned and her hips ground harder against his erection. Then he plunged his tongue deep into her mouth.

Nick wanted her naked and writhing on the bed, to see her offered up before him like a virgin sacrifice of old. He propped two pillows under her shoulders and pulled back, stripping her skirt, hose and panties down her legs at the same time.

The sudden loss of his body heat and her clothing made her flinch and she tried to cover herself. "Let me see you, Lila."

"This feels…"

"Decadent?"

"No."

"Uncomfortable?"

"Uneven."

"Ah…"

"Take off your clothes, Camden."

"Not yet. I'm still in charge."

"Do I get a chance?"

"Yes."

"Five minutes?"

He nodded.

"I'm your willing slave."

"Spread your legs, Lila."

She moved them apart a little bit.

"Farther."

She did, but her hands still hovered over her breasts. She hesitated.

"Trust me," he said.

She did as he asked and lay before him as he'd imagined so many times. She was infinitely lovelier than any woman he'd ever seen. He wanted her so badly he knew he wouldn't last long.

He wanted to taste her from head to toe and lowered himself between her legs to do just that. He started at her left foot and worked his way slowly up her body, pausing to carefully bite behind her knee. At the apex of her thighs, he sucked on the skin so close to her center that he felt her humid warmth. He sucked until she moaned and lifted her hips from the bed.

When he moved on to sweeter flesh, he left behind a small mark. He wanted to leave more of them behind. He parted her silken flesh and bent to taste the pearl he'd revealed. Lila's breaths were quickening. Her flesh quivered when he blew across it and when he touched her lightly with his tongue, she cried out.

He felt her body's response to him, wanted to feel it on his most sensitive flesh. He thrust two fingers inside her and she welcomed him with a fierce clenching that made his arousal even fuller.

"I can't wait," he said.

"I can't either," she said.

He freed himself and thrust into her. She was still quaking from her earlier climax, and he waited for her to calm then began to build the tension within both of them again. He kissed her eyes and cheeks, the long length of her neck and the berry-hardened tips of her breasts.

He caressed her back and spine, finally cupping her buttocks in his hands and tilting her hips so that he could thrust deeper inside her. She lifted herself to him and he felt the minute contractions in her lower body around his most intimate flesh. It was like being caressed by the warmest, wettest glove. A red haze settled over him and he put his arms under her legs, bending them slowly back toward her body.

He stopped when she gasped. He could barely think, much less speak, but he had to know if she was okay. "Hurt?"

She shook her head. "Can you take more of me?" he asked.

She nodded and he pressed her legs back farther until she was completely open to him. He thrust deeper, deeper than he'd ever been before. He felt as if he were touching her womb and then he climaxed. He felt Lila's body clench around him again and their eyes locked as they shot together to the stars. It was a long, hard ride and it emptied him of his seed—rocking him to his very soul.

Ten

Lila knew that some dreams never came true. She'd spent her childhood searching for a father who never appeared. She'd spent her teenage years waiting for a white knight to rescue her from the cruel taunts of the other kids. She'd spent half her life waiting for Mr. Right—and he'd appeared out of the blue.

The lingering stickiness between her legs reminded her that Nick hadn't used a condom. She wasn't sure what that meant. Maybe he'd forgotten again, but she doubted it. The act of unprotected sex had to mean more to him than that.

She looked at the man lying still and quiet next to her in the dark. Their bodies were covered in a sheen of sweat and Lila didn't feel strong enough to move under the covers.

She shivered a little and Nick pulled her closer to his body, wrapping himself around her, cupping her buttocks in his palm and brushing his lips against her neck. She'd never felt so cherished, so vulnerable, so…loved.

But love wasn't something she trusted. It didn't lead to respectability but to passion-filled unions. Though his body protected her now, she'd never felt as exposed as she had earlier, when he'd been in control. Surrendering control had been difficult.

She stirred in his arms, needing their relationship to be equal. Needing to see if what he felt for her was on the same level as what she felt for him. Did he trust her enough to cede control?

Running her fingers down the line of hair on his chest, she tickled the spot right above his groin. His flesh hardened and she caressed him tenderly. His touch on her back changed from languid to inciting, sliding around to the front of her body, brushing his forefinger across her nipple until a delicious warmth gathered between her legs.

The sexual energy in the room rekindled, and she felt its pull. She knew that she was about to surrender to him once again. But she wanted, no, needed to be his equal tonight. She needed to know that this encounter wasn't going to be relegated to another affair with another woman in his mind. She needed to know that he felt for her what she felt for him.

She glanced up his long lean body. His eyes were

open and he studied her with an intensity that left her breathless.

"You rang?"

She wanted to feel what he did, that sense of surety in her partner that he had in her. She knew that the next few minutes would determine whether or not they'd both found something lasting. Knew that it was up to Nick to make the next move. Knew that she had to be brave enough to follow through.

"Nick, I want my five minutes," she said.

He stared at her, and her heart sank. He wasn't going to give up control for anything…not even her. He rubbed his jaw and looked away.

She felt what he wasn't saying. That her emotions were stronger than his. That she'd bared her soul, but his lay safely protected. That she loved him, but he didn't trust in that love enough to make himself vulnerable.

Suddenly her nakedness made her uncomfortable. She tugged on the sheets, trying to cover herself. She should leave. But she couldn't move right now. If she shifted in one direction she'd explode into a million pieces.

He touched her back, one finger moving slowly down the line of her spine. Then she felt the heat of his mouth in a slow, burning kiss just above the curve of her buttocks.

"Lila?"

She couldn't look at him. "Yes?"

"Okay."

At first she wasn't sure she'd heard him correctly, the word had been uttered so softly.

One glance at his eyes was all the confirmation she needed. She saw in them a light that she'd never seen before.

"On your back, Camden." She wanted to explore his body. Though they'd made love several times she'd always focused on her reactions. Loving Nick as she did, she wanted to find out what drove him over the edge.

"I'm yours to command."

The thrill of power went to her head, and she closed her eyes for a minute. But only a minute. She knelt next to him and realized that she didn't want him to be in the same position she'd been in. She wanted this to be equal, but different.

"On your knees."

He knelt next to her on the bed. She didn't need to tell him to spread his legs. The strength of his erection necessitated that. She drew her nails up the length of his thighs, teasing him by caressing him everywhere but on the hungry flesh that craved her touch.

If she'd learned one thing from Nick it was that waiting made the culmination so much sweeter. Leaning forward she bit his pectoral right above his flat nipple. He moaned.

She sucked lightly on his skin. His hands moved up to hold her to him. He rubbed his chest against her mouth. The hair over his muscles made her lips tingle. She moved down his body, tracing him with her mouth. He leaned back and spread his legs wider. She slid between them. She felt his hot erection brushing at her stomach and reached down to take him in her hand.

She stroked him a few times, then his hand on hers stilled the motion. "I'd rather be inside you when I climaxed."

"I'd rather have you there."

He lay back on the pillows and pulled her forward. Lila slid over him, bracing herself with her hands on his shoulders. Nick helped her to impale herself on him. She rode him carefully, unsure of herself in this position. Unsure of herself in the dominant role. But Nick, teeth gritted and eyes locked to hers, was letting her take the lead.

Each time she slid up on him, his hips rose slightly, when she slid back down, his fingers flexed on the bed and his hands moved toward her hips.

The slow sensuous moving was a delicious torture. But soon she wanted more and murmured, "Okay, control is yours again."

She realized she really only wanted his trust, not to take him as he'd taken her. Because, as he held her hips and thrust into her as if he couldn't get enough of her, she realized that what he felt for her was as intense as what she felt for him. She felt her climax coming, and then Nick's as he reached between their bodies to caress her more intimately.

Her entire body tensed, and she felt Nick's warmth deep inside her. As she lay down on his body, his strong arms wrapped around her, she knew she'd never sleep alone again. She knew that Nick was ready for a lifelong commitment. She smiled to herself and drifted off to sleep imagining living in his house as man and wife.

Nick felt as if every nerve in his body had been exposed last night. The sensuality exceeded even his fantasies, but the result was a shocking vulnerability he'd never felt before. He didn't like it.

Lila looked small and fragile in the morning light that spilled through the windows. Last night she'd been a match for him in the dark, but now she seemed too delicate for him and the life he'd led.

She stirred on the bed, and he climbed out before she awoke. Although his first instinct was to cradle her close and never let her go, he'd found that the things you held on to hardest were usually the ones that slipped most easily away.

He went into the bathroom, bracing his hands on the sink, and bowed his head. What had started out as one thing—seduction and thank you—had turned into a soul-baring experience that made him doubt his sanity.

He couldn't live with someone who brought him that close to his true self. He couldn't be with her night after night until she left and still survive.

It had been different with Amelia. She'd never breached his inner walls, and even if she'd survived the cancer, he'd never have been able to let her past them. He didn't think he could live with Lila seeing him at his softest, knowing the power she had over him.

He showered and shaved, and, when he emerged from the bathroom, he was no closer to figuring out what he was going to do next. One thing was certain, Lila and he could never live together.

He stopped as he entered his bedroom. Lila was sitting on the window seat overlooking the backyard. She wore only his discarded shirt. Her knees were held tight to her chest and her glorious blond hair fell in rumpled waves against her back.

She looked alone and scared. After last night, she deserved to wake up in the arms of her lover—not alone. But he'd been unable to stay. How was he going to tell her that they couldn't see each other anymore?

Wounding her went against the grain, but in this instance his own self-preservation won out. His survival had to be paramount. He cared deeply for Lila, but she would move on and love again. At least that's what he kept telling himself.

He walked across the room, stopping about ten feet away from her. She glanced over her shoulder. Her eyes were guarded, and there was no welcoming smile on her face.

"I'm…" He spread his hands. Damn, he hated these kinds of conversations. Not that he'd ever really had them. Amelia hadn't touched him as deeply as Lila did. His parents hadn't either.

"Scared?" she asked.

He shrugged. *Scared* wasn't a word he'd ever apply to himself and he didn't like hearing her use it. But he knew that he was running from her. Even rationalizing it didn't help.

Honesty seemed like the best option at the moment. "Not sure what to say."

"How about that we're great together and you can't imagine us living apart?" She stood up and the anger in those movements cut him deep. Carefully he looked at her, cataloging her features and her expression. This was his great gift to womanhood. Anger and disillusionment. He never wanted to forget this.

"That's not in the cards for us."

"It could be." She marched up to him and stood, arms akimbo, before him. The hem of his shirt lifted to the top of her thighs. His entire body tightened. He wanted to slide his hand up under that shirt, knowing she was naked and needing to touch her. He didn't know if he could stop himself.

He started to reach for her, imagining her soft skin under his touch. Imagining the return of the passion that had swept them away the night before. Realizing that nothing would ever again be the same between them.

She glared at his hand hanging in mid-air. He dropped it to his side, but Lila clasped it in her own. Her grip was cold and firm.

"Dammit, Nick. What happened?" Her eyes were

glassy and he knew she was fighting back tears. He felt like a big bully on the playground.

He didn't know how to put into words what was going through him. Didn't want to be vulnerable to her again even though he'd already been stripped to the soul in front of her. He owed her something, though, because he wasn't the only one who'd bared his innermost being last night.

"It was too intense."

"It *was* intense—and real."

"Not real. Life isn't made up of those moments. It's mundane living through a daily routine. Some of us are meant to make that journey together. Others are not."

She let his hand slide from hers. "I take it we're in the 'not' category?"

"I am. But Lila, you deserve a decent guy for a husband. I care about you so this isn't easy."

"What if I'm pregnant?"

"Of course, I'll do my duty to your child, Lila."

"Not marriage?"

"You know how I feel about marriage."

"Yes, I do. But I have to be honest here, Nick. It sounds like a cop-out."

"I wish it was. After Amelia died, something inside of me shut down. Work became my life and I'll tell you something, I don't think I'd ever want to go back to the way I felt those first six months after I buried my wife."

"If something were to happen to me would it hurt less if I wasn't your wife?"

He hated her perception. He couldn't answer this question. "I hope not."

"Help me understand this."

He took her hand and led her to the bed. He motioned for her to sit down but didn't sit next to her. "I've told you how it was growing up. My family wasn't much of one, but I'd always had this perfect image in my mind of what a family should be."

"The McKees?"

He nodded. "I had my shot with Amelia. But it wasn't perfect either. Our lives didn't mesh, and we never became a solid unit the way Buster's parents had been.

"After she died, I decided not to try again. I didn't just lose Amelia when cancer took her. Fate took my dreams, Lila. And you can't give them back to me."

"I'm not trying to."

"What do you want from me?"

"Not duty, for God's sake. You have to work at being happy. It doesn't just drop in your lap.

"Do you love me?" she asked suddenly, her eyes boring into him as if she were trying to reach his soul again.

"Lila…"

She stood and started gathering her clothing. She stalked to the bathroom door. "Fate didn't take your dreams, Nick."

He didn't say anything.

"You gave them away because you're too afraid of life to take even the simplest risk. Life is a rich morsel meant to be savored, not a fine meal put in storage until it's moldy and gray."

She stormed out the door, and he tried to pretend that her going was for the best, but he didn't feel the relief he'd expected to feel. Instead he felt empty and even more alone.

Two days later, on Monday morning, Lila wasn't sure of anything except that she couldn't go into the Colette offices today. She'd woken up this morning to discover her period had arrived. No baby. Keen disappointment rolled through her. She knew it was for the best, but it didn't stop the tears from burning in her eyes.

A part of her would have always treasured a small being that was both her and Nick. Her dreams of happily ever after with Nick were dashed, but she knew in her heart that someday she'd try again, because she wanted a husband and a family. Maybe she'd try it without love. Maybe Nick was on to something, and it wouldn't hurt as much if she kept her emotions uninvolved.

She cleaned her apartment from top to bottom, washing all of the linens twice. She'd been unable to sleep in her bed because she remembered the night Nick had spent there, remembered his strong body wrapped around her own. Therefore, she'd spent Saturday night on the couch and last night in the kitchen baking.

She now had seven loafs of pumpkin, apple and banana nut breads, as well as enough cookies for the entire population of Indiana. But she hadn't felt in control last night while she'd been baking. She'd been like a mime going through the motions.

She had to shake off the lethargy that was plaguing her. Part of her said it had only been two days and it was okay to wallow, but the other part, the part that was trying to protect her, said to move on. Pack up her homey little apartment and start over somewhere else.

Because she didn't think she was going to be able to return to Colette, Inc. She wasn't even sure she was going to be able to leave her apartment now that she'd been so open about her affair with Nick. And it was over.

She called the office and told them she wouldn't be in today. She knew she was going to have to face Nick, would have to work with him day in and out. But not today. Today she was going to take the bread and cookies to Charlotte and Myrtle at the seniors' center. Then she was going to do some thinking and make some choices about the future.

As much as Nick had hurt her, she knew that she'd been expecting him to. Knew that from the first time they'd made love on his desk, she'd been waiting for him to leave. Had known deep in her heart that a vice president wouldn't settle for his secretary.

She checked her watch to make sure Nick would be in the weekly staff meeting before dialing his private line. She had to let him know that she wasn't pregnant.

His voicemail clicked on and Lila wasn't sure what to say. "Hi, it's Lila. I'm not—you don't—"

She hit the command to delete the message before he received it. This obviously wasn't something she could say over the phone. Maybe she'd send him an e-mail.

She finished getting dressed, realizing she still had Rose's pin. It hadn't brought her luck or love, she thought. It was probably time to return it to Rose.

She caressed the amber-and-metal jewel. The heart-shaped design drew her eye and romantic interest. She wondered who'd designed the brooch. It took a special person to design something that went beyond jewelry and became art.

Tucking the brooch into her coat pocket, she packed her baked goods in a large basket. She packed a smaller basket for Mr. McKee. She'd learned from Charlotte that he was back at home with a round-the-clock nurse. She didn't examine her motives too carefully, but she knew that although she was angry with Nick, right now she'd never be able to cut Nick out of her life. The people who were important to him would always be important to her.

The phone rang as she was leaving and she waited for the machine to pick up.

"Lila, are you home?"

Nick's voice echoed through her apartment, sending tingles of awareness down her spine. He sounded tired and frustrated.

He sighed. "I need to talk to you. If you don't pick up I'm going to come over and wait outside your window. I think we're too old for those kind of games but if you want to play I think you should know I always win."

His words didn't scare her. She was leaving. She could stay gone until he gave up and went home, but that was a childish thing to do. What she felt for Nick, what they'd had together, deserved more than that. She picked up the handset. "Nick?"

"Thought that would get you to talk."

"I'm not playing a childish game, Nick. I just need time to adjust."

"I know. I wanted to make sure you're okay."

"I am," she said, knowing she should tell him she wasn't pregnant, but the words wouldn't come.

"I've done some thinking since our discussion," he said.

"About?"

"What you said. I realized I'm not the only one who's running."

Damn, she thought. "I was willing to stop for you."

"It felt like you only slowed down."

"What's that supposed to mean?"

"Only that you never trusted me to stay, did you?"

"Hey, I loved you."

"Past tense already, Lila? It's only been two days."

"Well, being shown the door does that to a woman."

"Being judged and found wanting does that to a man."

"I didn't judge you."

"You sure as hell did. Why else all the secrecy and sneaking around?"

"I never asked you to sneak," she said, avoiding what she was beginning to believe was the truth.

"Not with words, but with actions."

Silence buzzed along the open line and Lila couldn't breathe for a minute.

"I tried to give you everything I had," she said quietly and hung up the phone.

It rang again almost immediately and Lila hurried out the door, but not before she heard Nick's deep voice once more through her answering machine. She knew she was running but realized that this time she wasn't running away. She'd made a good life for herself in Youngsville, and she wasn't about to give it up along with the only man she'd ever loved.

Eleven

The board meeting was long and boring, and Nick didn't pay much attention to anything that was said. Which concerned him. Colette had saved his life after Amelia died, and here he was letting his job performance slide.

The meeting adjourned, and Xavier stopped him in the hall. "I wanted to thank your secretary for defending the board and the choices we make."

Xavier had his hand in many pies at Colette and information was one of the areas that he exceeded at. But still, how could he have heard about cafeteria gossip? "Lila is very loyal to Colette. But how did you get wind of her actions?"

"My assistant was in the cafeteria. You know

many of our staff are playing the wait-and-see game, but she isn't. She's a fine woman.''

Xavier's words made him feel like a bastard because he knew they were true. ''You've never met her, Xavier. Maybe she was hedging her bets.''

''Do you think so?'' Xavier asked.

Nick had a brief idea that he should plant a seed in Xavier's mind and then go ahead and fire Lila. It wasn't a noble thing to do, but he was at a loss as to how to deal with her after she'd seen him at his lowest. But he'd also seen her at her lowest and that made him want to protect her.

Nick shook his head. ''No. She wouldn't do that. She's very loyal and involved in the success of Colette. I've never worked with a finer person—man or woman.''

Xavier put his hand on Nick's shoulder. The two men had known each other a long time and Nick knew that Xavier had helped save his sanity after Amelia's death. ''There's been a lot of tension around the office lately, and you've been putting in too many hours. Why don't you take the afternoon off?''

Where would he go? He had nothing outside of the office to turn to. He'd driven away the one woman who might have been interested in filling those empty hours. ''My work is my life, Xavier.''

His boss looked at him shrewdly and Nick thought he might have come up lacking. ''Maybe it shouldn't be.''

Xavier walked away, and Nick went back to his

own office. He knew that work wasn't his life any-more; that he couldn't let it be if he wanted to survive. But the leap he'd have to take to make that change seemed impossible.

And he knew he'd have to make a change.

Wishing wouldn't make his office situation any different. He and Lila were going to have to move forward and the more he thought about it the less he liked the idea of her not sitting in his outer office. But more than that, he disliked the thought of their lives not intermingling. Of her house not being his, her life not overlapping his, her children not being his.

Damn, he'd forgotten to ask her about the pregnancy test when he'd talked to her earlier. The way he'd acted he wouldn't have blamed her if she hadn't told him. Hell, he wasn't too sure he'd have told him-self.

His office reminded him of Lila. Of them making love and more. Her spunk and attitude when he'd behaved in a way that no new lover should. She was his match on so many levels.

She was too good for him, for the bitter lonely man he'd let life shape him into. He thought he might want to be better for her, but those kinds of decisions weren't ones taken lightly. Maybe it was only the lust talking. He'd never had a lover to equal Lila. And it wasn't only physical. Something else happened be-tween them when they made love.

She'd shared her dreams with him. Images of a

future where she lived in a large house with a white picket fence and had a family. A real family, with a husband and kids. Something he'd never offered her. He'd shared his lonely vision of the world where parents hated each other and the child grew up distrustful.

The very things she needed were things he'd never been able to depend on, but he knew that he was going to have to or he'd lose her forever. On Saturday morning, when they'd parked, he'd wanted only to get away from her, to hide in the dark until his protective skin had had time to regenerate. But now, with the distance of time, he realized that she hadn't peeled that layer away. He'd let it drop and invited her in without ever realizing it.

The threat to Colette had made one thing abundantly clear in his life. The job couldn't be all he had. He needed more. He closed his eyes. The only woman he could see by his side as his wife was Lila Maxwell.

"Damn," he muttered. Convincing her to stay with him was going to be hard. Could he change the habits of a lifetime? He didn't think so. But he knew he wasn't going to be responsible for making her cry again.

Nick remembered the night they'd gone to the symphony and his words, *I wish I could watch over you.* What an ass he'd been. Could he have tried any harder to push her away?

Even Xavier believed that his job wasn't important to him anymore. Of course, he wasn't going to let any hostile takeover wrest control of Colette without a fight, but his heart wasn't in it as much as it had once been.

His heart wasn't even his own anymore. It belonged to Lila. But he was afraid to give it to her.

He put his elbows on his desk and dropped his forehead into his hands, closing his eyes against the burn of tears. How could he love her? He knew nothing about happily ever after. But what he felt was so extreme it could only be love.

This should be the happiest moment of his life. His heart was pounding, and he knew he'd have to figure out a way to get her to stay without revealing his feelings. Those were words he could never say out loud. Never even intimate that he might have deep emotions for her.

He'd never survive if something happened to her and he didn't know what the future held. Didn't know what he was going to do because he couldn't live with Lila and he'd only just realized how barren life would be without her.

Lila left the seniors' center after a nice visit with Myrtle and Charlotte. Afterwards, she'd located Mr. McKee's apartment, but he wasn't up to visitors so she left the basket she'd made for him with his attendant. Seeing the elderly man lying pale on the bed made her heart ache. Not for herself, but for Nick.

As much as she'd wanted to cling to the bitterness he'd inspired in her, she couldn't. She loved him. At this moment it hurt like hell, but the pain reminded her she was still alive.

The day was gray, cloudy and cold. A light rain fell as she stepped outside. She pulled her gloves from her pocket and wrapped her muffler around her throat.

"Lila?"

She pivoted to see Buster McKee behind her. "Hi, Buster."

"Is Nick here with you?"

She shook her head. This was the beginning, she realized, the beginning of life without someone whom you'd made important. Though they had been together for only a month, she felt as if their lives were inexplicably entwined.

"I wanted to thank him again for all he's done for Dad."

"He wouldn't want your thanks. He did it out of kindness. Your dad is important to him," Lila said, though she figured Buster already knew that.

"I know. You had to see his parents to really appreciate your own."

"Tell me about them," she said, knowing she was using false pretenses to learn more about Nick. But maybe Buster could give her some insight that Nick simply couldn't.

"They looked like a perfect family on the outside, you know. I mean his mom was a CPA and his dad was a lawyer, and in public they presented this family that was straight out of *Saturday Evening Post*."

"And they weren't." Nick had said that the face of the enemy wasn't one he wanted to see in her.

"Maybe they were. But those two, they should never have had kids. They made Nick's life tough and I know he did whatever it took to graduate from high school early and go to college.

"His parents told him he was unlovable. That if he'd been a different child, his life could have been better."

Lila shivered in the rain, and she wished she could wrap her arms around Nick and hold him to her. To make him understand that he was so much more than his parents made him believe he was.

"When I saw the basket you dropped off for Dad, well, it made me realize that Nick had finally found someone who could love him as he deserved."

She could only stare at him, tears burning the back of her eyes. How could she tell him that she could love Nick with her heart and soul, but he'd never accept it? Now that she knew about Nick's past and finally understood what his formative years had been like, she realized that the secret hope she'd been harboring that he'd come back to her was self-delusion.

"I better let you get out of the rain."

Lila only nodded as she watched Buster leave. Her head down, she hurried to her car. The cold wet day was a perfect match for the weeping she was doing inside.

The key jammed in the door of her car, a domestic sedan that had seen better days and that she'd been reluctant to get rid of after it had made the trip to Indiana.

She sat in the parking lot for a few minutes waiting for the car to warm up. Her mind was full of Buster's voice telling her things about Nick's past. Nick's voice telling her that he never wanted to wake up and see her as his enemy. Her voice telling him he had to learn to love.

Turning up the volume on her radio to drown out the sound of the voices, she flipped channels, searching for the right song. Something loud, she thought. Not the Chili Peppers or Creed because they'd make her think. She found the local jazz station and raised the volume even more.

She put the car in Drive and realized as she was driving that it had started to snow. In Florida, snow had seemed romantic and fun, everything that fall and winter should be. Last winter she'd had a minor fender-bender while driving in the stuff.

She slowed her car and drove sedately toward town. The deejay introduced a recording of classic jazz...Lena Horne's *Someone To Watch Over Me*. Lila's foot slipped off the gas before she remembered where she was.

She put her foot more securely on the pedal and reached for the radio dial to change it. Remembering her own mother's melancholy reaction to that song was one thing, actually letting sadness seep through herself was something else.

She hit an icy patch on the road and her car did a

360°-loop. Everything spun so quickly. She tried to steer into it but she had no control. She slammed forward as her car rocked to a stop and impacted a tree.

Her head hit the steering wheel before the seatbelt yanked her back and the airbag exploded in her face. She slumped forward in her seat. The music still played in her mind and the voices continued to swirl around. Her heart felt heavy and her future looked dim as pictures of her life flashed in her mind. She had an image of herself and Nick as they'd looked the night they'd attended the symphony. Her mother and her at the beach. Nick and she in her bed, the desperate way he'd held her close. Nick's face as she'd seen it that last time.

Her head pounded, and she couldn't keep her eyes open. Pinpricks of light, so bright she couldn't focus clearly on them, floated around her and she gave up consciousness wishing for Nick and the life they could have shared.

Nick was leaving the office when the receptionist stopped him to take a call.

"Take a message," he requested.

"She said it was an emergency, Mr. Camden."

He took the phone from the receptionist and barked his name into it.

"I'm sorry to bother you. This is Kitty Maxwell, Lila's mother."

"Yes, ma'am?" Nick suddenly felt sick to his stomach.

"She's been in an accident. I'm on my way to the airport, but I won't be able to get to Indiana until late tonight. Will you go to the hospital and wait with her?"

"Don't worry, ma'am. I'll take care of her."

He hung up the phone and left the building as fast as he could. He drove as quickly and safely through town as possible, knowing that nothing could stop Fate. If Lila lived, she would whether he was sitting by her side or not. But he wanted to be by her side. Needed to be there so that he could give her some of his strength.

He parked and ran inside, not sure what he'd find. The emergency room was busy but not too crowded. He approached a reception desk, introduced himself as Lila's fiancé and was directed to a small curtained-off area. Lila sat on the side of the bed. A huge bandage covered most of her forehead and her fingers were laced tightly together.

"I'm going home, doctor," she said, her voice hoarse and small but determined.

"No, miss, you are not, not unless you have someone to take care of you."

"I will," Nick said. He wanted to make a vow to her there in the hospital because seeing her made him want to protect her always.

Lila glanced at him, but there was no welcome in her eyes. No wild emotions that called to his soul and made him want to react to her. Nothing that showed he was anything to her other than a boss.

"And you are?" the doctor asked.

"My boss," Lila said.

Her boss. Nick wanted to argue that he was so much more, but knew he'd forfeited the right. He'd forced Lila out of her comfort zone and challenged her to acknowledge him as her lover, and then pushed her away. Sometimes he really could be a bastard.

"She has a mild concussion. Here's a prescription for the pain, and she needs to be awakened every four hours," the doctor instructed Nick.

Nick pocketed the prescription. The doctor left them alone in the curtained room. It smelled of cleaner and antiseptic. Next door someone moaned in pain, and a doctor was paged over the loudspeaker.

"What are you doing here?" Lila asked. Her tone held a hint of accusation, almost as if she didn't believe he deserved to be there. Maybe he didn't.

"Your mom asked me to come."

"Well, you've fulfilled your duty. Thanks for getting rid of the doc but, I'm fine from here out."

"How are you planning to get home?"

"I'll take the bus."

"You are so stubborn."

"I'm not the only one."

He glared at her, realizing that she called to the extremes in him. Lila was never going to be a safe placid lover. She was always challenging him, not just to be his best but to be on his toes.

"Let's get you home."

She didn't say anything else. An aura of fragility

surrounded her, and he was afraid even to touch her. But he knew he had to. He wanted to feel her breath against his neck and her heartbeat under his hands to affirm that she was whole and fine.

He pulled her into his arms and held her for a minute realizing how desperately happy he was that she was alive and only concussed. She held herself stiff in his arms and then slowly, when he didn't let go, she wrapped her arms around his waist and rested her head on his chest.

He brushed her hair back from her face, placing the smallest of kisses right next to the white bandage. Her breath caught and she pulled away.

"I can't do this, Nick. Not now."

She was right. He needed to get her out of the hospital, and she needed rest. Then they could talk and touch. Because he wasn't going to feel as though she was safe until he could just hold her in his arms. Then he was going to have to convince her that what they had would last. He knew now that it would.

"Stay here, I'll see what we have to do for you to leave."

"Where am I going to go?"

"Don't be smart with me," he said.

She just shook her head, and he remembered the way she'd been after they'd made love on his desk. Her sass was her defense mechanism and he couldn't blame her for it. After all, he'd shown her that he was her enemy.

"I'm not your enemy anymore," he said.

"We'll see," she said.

She closed her eyes. Nick knew she wasn't up to a conversation. He walked out without saying anything else. He found the doctor, and Lila signed a few papers and then they left. He wanted to carry her, but she glared at him when he suggested it.

He seated her in his car. "Your house or mine?"

"Amber Court, please."

"My place is closer," he said.

"Nick, I don't want to go to your home."

He said nothing else, just drove quietly toward her place. He drove through the twenty-four-hour pharmacy and dropped off Lila's prescription.

When they arrived at her place, he parked on the street and came around to open her door. She was glaring at him again and Nick knew he'd made a big mistake, one that he was going to have to continue to pay for unless he made some changes.

He scooped her up into his arms, kicked the door closed and crossed the street. The rain had changed to a light flurry of snow and it dusted Lila's hair and clothing, making her look even more like an angel.

He entered the marble foyer and Rose Carson, Lila's landlady, came out, saying in shocked tones, "Lila, are you okay?"

"She has a mild concussion. I'm going to take care of her," said Nick.

Rose smiled slightly and murmured, "Good."

She went back into her apartment, and Nick felt as if he'd been given a seal of approval.

"Maybe I wanted Rose to stay with me."

"Looks like you're stuck with me," he said.

"Nick—"

"Not here in the hallway, okay?"

She nodded, and he carried her up to her apartment and placed her on the bed. Nick helped her remove her boots and coat. He wanted to help her change into her nightgown, but she was already asleep when he removed her second boot. He pulled the covers over her.

Lila's mother called to say that she couldn't get a flight until the next day, and Nick assured her that he was staying with Lila and she'd be okay. He hung up and took off his own coat, shoes and belt. He set his watch alarm for four hours and climbed into bed next to her, pulling her into his arms. He couldn't sleep, but holding her brought him a peace he hadn't realized he'd been searching for.

Twelve

Lila rolled over in her sleep, waking when she realized that Nick's arms were around her. She wondered where all of his protectiveness was coming from. Why did he suddenly seem not to want to let her out of his sight?

But she welcomed it. She felt puny today. The wound on her head throbbed, and her body had a bunch of bruises on it. She was acutely aware of every place their bodies touched and she snuggled closer to him while he was sleeping and couldn't see how much she needed him, needed his touch.

She stared at his face so close to hers. Even in sleep his intensity didn't wane. He looked fierce as he held her. She traced one finger lightly over his features.

She'd never noticed the small scar under his right eye. She memorized his features and the security his arms brought her, knowing that once he was awake and out of bed, she'd never touch him again.

She had to tell him there was no baby. Had to let him know that there was no reason for him to protect her. Had to make sure he knew his obligations to her were over.

His eyes opened and she found herself staring into his deep-blue eyes. They always reminded her of the Atlantic Ocean near the Keys where her mother used to take her every summer when she was a little girl.

"Lila? Are you okay?" he asked.

"Yes, I'm fine." But the words were a lie. She'd never be fine again. And she didn't know how to make his life right for him, knowing she wasn't the one who should do it anyway.

She glanced at the clock. It was 7:00 a.m. The sun peeked though the edges of her wooden blinds. It looked like it was going to be a nice day. She vaguely recalled Nick waking her throughout the night.

"Thanks for staying with me last night."

"No problem. I, um, had to sleep with you because the couch is too small."

She wanted to tease him about that, the way she would have a few days earlier, but now she didn't know where they stood. She knew she had a secret she had to share and that he'd told her she was running from life the last time they talked. So much was unsettled between them. She was almost afraid to settle it because then he'd leave and she'd be alone again, spending all of her nights dreaming of a man she couldn't have.

"Why don't you wash up and I'll fix you some breakfast?" Nick stood and she realized he'd slept in his clothes, too.

"Okay," she said, wanting to delay the moment when she had to tell him they weren't having a baby. Delay the moment when she'd sever the last bond between them. Delay the moment when he left for good.

She grabbed a change of clothes and walked to the bathroom. "Don't lock the door in case you fall."

"Will you catch me?" she asked before she could stop herself.

"I will," he said and walked to the kitchen.

She showered and dressed and joined him in her small kitchen. He'd made coffee and found some waffles she'd frozen the week before.

They sat at her counter to eat. When he finished his breakfast, he stood. "Ready to talk?"

She nodded.

"Let's go sit in the living room."

Her couch was comfortable, and Nick hadn't really spent a lot of time there. She didn't want him sitting on it now. Didn't want to have another piece of furniture or another room in her house that was overwhelmed by the memory of him.

But she sat next to him just the same. "I..."

"Lila, please let me say something first."

"Okay."

He swallowed and stood to pace the room. "You were right when you said that I was hiding from life and that Fate wasn't responsible, I was."

She wrapped her arms around her waist to keep from going to him and pulling him into her embrace. She knew it was duty that motivated him to speak to her.

"I've always known you were smart."

He didn't smile as she'd hoped.

"Lila, all my life I've been searching for something that was just out of my reach. Ambition in my career brought me close, my marriage to Amelia brought me closer, but neither of them touched the part of me that you did."

"I'm not sure that I really could reach you, Nick."

"I didn't know it either until I came so close to losing you."

"I was already lost to you. You said it. I was running away from love again."

"No, you weren't. This time I drove you away. I don't know about the past and I really don't care about it. I've always lived for the future and I want that future to include you and our baby."

Finally, he knelt at her feet, arms caging her hips and pulled her toward him. He lowered his head so that it rested against her stomach. She wanted to wrap her arms around him and hold him to her, but she knew he'd leave when she told him what she needed to say. Had to say it now.

"Nick…"

"Shh," he said, covering her lips with his fingers. "I know I've been cruel in the past, but as of this moment forward my life belongs to you. I can't live without you."

He straightened from her body and took her left hand in his. He caressed her fingers before lowering his head and brushing a butterfly-soft kiss against her hand. She shivered and watched him.

"Will you marry me?"

The words she'd always wanted to hear from the man who owned her body, heart and soul. The tears that had been burning the back of her eyes since he dropped to his knees in front of her began to fall.

"I can't," she said.

"Why not?"

"I'm not pregnant, Nick. There's no reason for us to marry."

Lila stood and stalked to the window. She stared blindly down at the street, wrapping her arms around herself and holding tight. Waiting for the inevitable sound of Nick leaving. Though she'd been expecting it, the sound of his footsteps still lanced through her, making the tears fall.

Nick knew he was probably going to rot in hell for what he'd done to Lila. He deserved to pay for the mess he'd made of both of their lives. All he'd really wanted to do was love her and yet that had gone awry.

Of course, he'd been hedging when he'd asked her

to marry him. Trying to protect himself and not give her a way out, and still she'd found one. An unexpected one that hurt him as much as it hurt her.

Lingering fear from his childhood made him believe that he was the wrong man for her, but sometime during the night as they'd slept close to each other in her bed, he'd come to realize that Lila and he were meant for each other. He'd dreamed of them in a house with a white picket fence and children playing in the yard. He'd dreamed of her pregnant with their third child and him holding her while a large group of their family and friends surrounded them.

He'd dreamed of a life he'd never had a shot at before her, and he wasn't going to let that slip through his fingers now. He'd waited a lifetime to find the woman of his dreams, not even realizing that he'd been searching for her.

He stepped out to Lila, and she stiffened when he touched her back. His hand seemed too big and rough for Lila in her pretty pink sweater. Should he leave? He heard the small catch in her throat as she breathed, knew she was crying and that he was responsible for those tears.

He pulled her into his arms. Her back pressed solidly to his front, he held her tightly and brushed his mouth against her ear. There were words he had to say, but he could do no more than whisper them.

She sniffled, and he reached for a tissue and carefully dried her face. She wouldn't turn in his arms, but in the window he saw their reflections. His big, dark shape behind her smaller one. They looked like yin and yang and he realized they were.

Man without woman, woman without man was not how nature intended humans to live. Until that moment he hadn't acknowledged why he needed Lila in his life, but finally he could.

"I love you," he said. They were words he'd never said before, not even to Amelia, who'd been a good friend and someone he'd cared deeply about.

She turned in his embrace. Her gaze searched his face and silent tears tracked down her pale cheeks. He brushed them away with a kiss, the salty taste of her tears bittersweet to his tongue.

He leaned back and she framed his face with her hands. Then leaning up on her toes, she pulled his mouth to hers. He kissed her with the care of a man who knows that he's finally found what he's spent his life searching for. Kissed her as if she were water and he'd spent the last years in the desert. Kissed her with all the emotion he'd been hiding from.

"Marrying you is about the only thing that can save me from a long, lonely life. Lila, you've been telling me that I threw my dreams away—but you've made me dream again."

"You're sure?" she asked, when he pulled back to breathe.

"Yes." He'd never been surer of anything. Even though he felt almost weak at the thought of putting himself in her hands. "Believe me, I love you."

"I love you, too."

Her words made him strong. And he realized that loving wasn't something that weakened you. It was something that made you stronger.

"I wanted your baby so badly."

"We'll have lots of babies," he said. He realized his dream last night hadn't only been a nice image of the future. It had been a warning that he was letting his destiny slip through his fingers.

"If this is a dream, don't wake me," she whispered.

Her words sealed it. "It's not a dream, Florida girl. It's Fate, and you can't escape it."

"I guess Rose's pin worked after all."

"What pin?"

"The heart-shaped brooch I've been wearing. Rose said it would bring me luck and love."

"Is that what it brought you?" he asked.

"It brought to life the desires I'd been hiding from."

"Which ones? Because I thought I had something to do with those physical desires."

"You did. This brooch woke me up and made me realize I'd spent all my nights dreaming of you."

His throat closed, and he hugged her fiercely to his chest. She held him with just as much strength. Nick brushed his lips against her ear and murmured, "Me, too."

"You're sure?" she asked.

"Positive." He knew that although she said she

hadn't been looking for someone to watch over her, she'd found someone all the same.

"Then take me to bed and hold me close."

Nick swept her up in his arms and carried her to the bed. "I'm going to make certain that you never have to settle for dreams again, Lila. You've got the real thing by your side for the rest of your days."

"The real thing is so much better than dreams."

"Let me prove it to you."

Her smile said yes. He laid her on the rumpled covers and placed himself next to her.

The intensity he always felt when he was with Lila was tempered with a new peace he'd never known before. Their mouths engaged in long, slow kisses, kindling a fire that burned through them both.

He joined their hands together and their eyes met, silently acknowledging the deep and lasting bond they'd made with their lives.

Two days later Lila returned the brooch to Rose. She and Nick had just returned from dropping off her mom at the airport. Lila had been pleased at how well her mom and Nick had gotten along. The minute her mother had seen Nick she'd hugged him close. When they'd announced their engagement, she'd told him to call her Mom.

"Thanks for loaning me this pin, Rose."

"You're welcome. Did it bring you luck?"

"It brought me more than that."

"Good, I think I may lend it to Meredith. She's a little nervous about going on the auction block."

Lila thought her friend was more than a little nervous. "Good idea."

"You look better today," Rose said.

"I feel incredible. You can be one of the first to know. Nick and I are getting married."

"Congratulations, dear."

"Thank you," Lila said.

Lila went back upstairs and found Nick sitting alone at the kitchen table. "What are you working on?"

He tugged her onto his lap and kissed her with an intensity that usually ended up with them both naked. But not today. They were going to drive out and visit Mr. McKee and Charlotte and Myrtle.

He pulled back and reached around her to show her a piece of paper. "I was thinking about Rose's brooch and I want to commission a similar piece for you."

Her throat closed. "I can think of nothing I'd love more."

"Not even me?" he asked, the words light, but she knew he still wasn't as secure as he should be.

"I love nothing more than you."

He pulled her close, his face buried against his neck. "I just want some of this luck for our children."

"Me, too," she said. They sat quietly talking about the future and the brooch. They knew that their bond would be strong enough to see them through the ups and downs of life and that they'd both found the one thing they'd never have had on their own…true love.

* * * * *

Turn the page for a sneak preview
of the next 20 AMBER COURT *title,*

THE BACHELORETTE
by rising star Kate Little
on sale November 2001 in
Silhouette Desire...

And don't miss any of the books in the
20 AMBER COURT *series,*
only from Silhouette Desire:

WHEN JAYNE MET ERIK,
September 2001
by Elizabeth Bevarly

SOME KIND OF INCREDIBLE,
October 2001
Katherine Garbera

THE BACHELORETTE,
November 2001
by Kate Little

RISQUÉ BUSINESS,
December 2001
by Anne Marie Winston

One

The morning had been absolutely exasperating—even for a Monday, Meredith decided. She'd missed the bus and gotten caught in a downpour without an umbrella. Not to mention a run in her panty hose that was now as wide as the mighty Mississippi.

She scurried from the elevator to her office, opened the door and slipped inside.

Usually, a little rain or a ruined stocking wouldn't phase her. Her appearance was always neat, but carefully planned to blend into the woodwork. But she was due to give a presentation this morning to just about every high-level person in the company. Meredith dreaded speaking to groups, or any situation that put her in the limelight. Having her hair and outfit wrecked by the rain made the job even worse.

With her office door firmly closed behind her, she worked on some basic repairs, starting with her long reddish-brown hair, which was matted and damp, curling in every direction at once. She brushed it back tightly in her usual style, a simple ponytail secured with a clip. A bit severe perhaps, but certainly practical. Her complexion was fair, with faint freckles on her nose. She rarely tried to cover them with make-up. In fact, she usually wore no make-up at all. Which was just as well, she thought, since this morning she'd definitely have a bad case of raccoon eyes from melted mascara.

Her large blue eyes stared black at her in the mirror from behind oversize, tortoise-shell frames. She removed the glasses and wiped the damp lenses with a tissue. She often wished she could wear contact lenses, and had several pairs in her medicine chest. But her eyes never felt truly comfortable in contacts, especially during the close work required for jewelry design. Besides, she had no one special to impress.

A long floral skirt hid most of the run in her hose, she noticed. But her baize, V-neck sweater top, usually so baggy and figure concealing, now clung damply to her body like a second skin. Her mother had often told her that her ample curves on top were a blessing, but Meredith had never felt that way. To the contrary, she felt quite self-conscious about her busty physique and the unwanted attention it brought her, especially from men. Unlike most women she knew, Meredith did all she could to hide her curves, rather than show them off.

The large brooch pinned to her sweater pulled on the wet fabric and Meredith carefully unfastened the clasp. She took a moment to study the pin, holding it carefully in the palm of her hand. It was amazingly unique. Anyone would notice that. As a jewelry designer, it seemed even more remarkable to Meredith. It was a one-of-a-kind item you might come upon in an ''arty'' shop of handmade jewelry, or in a place that handled estate sales and antique pieces. Meredith's landlady, Rose Carson, had given it to her last night, when she'd been down at Rose's apartment having coffee. Rose was wearing the pin and Meredith had admired it. Then, without any warning at all, Rose took the pin off and offered it to her, insisting that Meredith borrow it for a while.

''Rose, it's lovely. But it must be very precious to you... What if I lose it?'' Meredith had asked.

''Don't be silly, you won't lose it,'' Rose had insisted. ''Here, put it on,'' Rose said, helping Meredith with the clasp. ''Let's see how it looks.''

Meredith had to agree it looked stunning. Yet she felt uncomfortable borrowing such a valuable piece of jewelry. But Rose, in her gracious, gentle way, wouldn't take no for an answer.

The design was roughly circular, a hand-worked base of different precious metals, studded with chunks of amber and polished gemstones. Staring down at it now in her hand, Meredith still found the composition fascinating, almost magically mesmerizing if one stared at it long enough, with the interplay of glittering jewels of so many different colors, shapes and cuts. The flickering shards of light thrown off from the jewels made Meredith feel almost lightheaded and she had to look away to regain her bearings. She had the oddest feeling each time she studied the pin, she noticed. But she couldn't quite understand why.

Brushing the question aside, she slipped the pin into the deep pocket of her skirt, feeling sure it would be safe there. Rose claimed the pin always brought her luck, and Meredith hoped that it would work for her today at her presentation, even hidden away in her pocket.

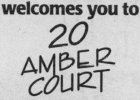

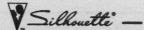
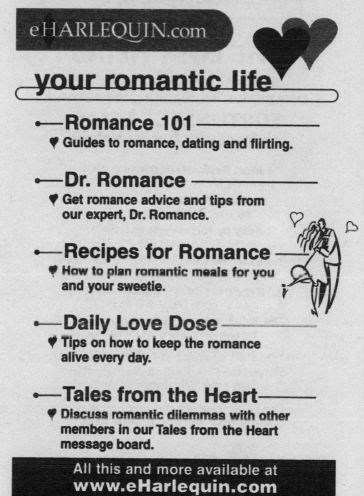

Silhouette Books cordially invites you to come
on down to Jacobsville, Texas, for

DIANA PALMER's
LONG, TALL TEXAN
Weddings

(On sale November 2001)

The LONG, TALL TEXANS series from international
bestselling author Diana Palmer is cherished around the
world. Now three sensuous, charming love stories from
this blockbuster series—*Coltrain's Proposal, Beloved* and
"Paper Husband"—are available in one special volume!

*As free as wild mustangs, Jeb, Simon and Hank vowed
never to submit to the reins of marriage. Until, of course,
a certain trio of provocative beauties tempt these Lone Star
lovers off the range...and into a tender, timeless embrace!*

**You won't want to miss
LONG, TALL TEXAN WEDDINGS
by Diana Palmer, featuring two
full-length novels and one short story!**

Available only from Silhouette Books at your favorite retail outlet.

Silhouette®
Where love comes alive™